Norton's Tale

A Skunk Tales Trilogy Book

Dylan Weiss

Red Engine Press
Pittsburgh, Pennsylvania

ISBN Trade Paperback: 978-1-943267-40-8
ISBN E-book: 978-1-943267-41-5
Library of Congress Control Number: 2017938438

Cover designed by Sandi Linhart
Edited by Betsy Beard

Printed in the United States.
Red Engine Press

Dedication

Norton's Tale is dedicated to my most treasured and beloved grandchildren: Joey and his sister Dylan, Samantha and her brother Jordan, who inspire me by their youthful exuberance, innocence, and love.

"*I learned this, at least, by my experiment; that if one advances confidently in the direction of his dreams, and endeavors to live the life which he has imagined, he will meet with a success unexpected in common hours.*"

Henry David Thoreau, Walden

~ 1 ~

The Skunk Norton Bulymer

Fall came early to the ancient lands of Eastphalia and Westphalia. It was late September and already the trees had shed their leaves, leaving a colorful carpet on the forest floor. Bare branches shivered against a chilly wind, and the whiff of forest decay heralded the coming of winter. That year would prove to be a historic one, thereafter known as the Year of the Skunk Salvation Seekers.

The change in seasons affected all animals. There was organization and harmony in how, to-gether, they all survived with the help of Mother Nature herself. Birds that could not survive the cold flew to warmer climates. Bears found caves in which to hibernate. And the fur of the weasel turned from brown to white, a camouflage against ene-mies—just one example of how Mother Nature gave each of her beloved animals a means of protection.

In those days, the animals were well protected... that is, all except for one. At great risk was the striped skunk, relative of the brown-in-summer, white-in-winter weasel. For some reason, Mother

Nature had overlooked skunks, providing only a simple threat behavior in their defense arsenal. Skunks stomped their front feet in the presence of an enemy, but unfortunately for skunks, stomping did little to stave off hungry predators.

Norton Bulymer was the most unfortunate in the unfortunate family of skunks, for he had an even greater predicament. Norton was the first in his family to have been born with a rare genetic defect—no stripes. So once winter came, and the landscape became a backdrop of bright white, Norton was at a terrible disadvantage. With his shiny black pelt he became an obvious target, darting through the snow. Norton's flawed fur was the bane of his existence, so much so that as a child he began dabbling in chemistry, always seeking a solution to the deformity that left him stripped of his stripes. Now a credentialed chemist, Norton worked feverishly in his laboratory. First he needed to find the honor, recognition, and dignity that other skunks were born with. Second, since snow was not far off, Norton needed camouflage, not wanting to suffer the perils of previous winters. Those skunk stripes were vital both to Norton's self-esteem and his self-preservation.

* * *

It was almost dawn when Norton stumbled upon an unusual outcropping of rock. It was dark brown and sooty in appearance, with white veins running throughout. After digging out some of the new rock to take home to his laboratory, Norton lay down and went to sleep, overcome by exhaustion. When he awoke, the sun was just beginning to set. Norton raced toward home, excited to get back to the lab and begin another experiment. By the time he reached his burrow, it was half past dusk.

"Thank heavens I'm back. It's a miracle I haven't already ended up dinner for some owl."

Norton lifted his paws high into the air and beseechingly asked Mother Nature, "Why did you leave me unprotected and without distinction? Even my weasel cousin, Mordecai, will be camouflaged." Then he shrugged in discouragement. "Everyone blends in, all except for me."

Norton entered his lab, which took up most of the main room of his burrow. He noted, as always, that the air was heavy with the pungent odor of chemicals, the result of years of trial, error, and determination. Test tubes contained different kinds of steaming, bubbling, and boiling tonics.

Norton slowly scanned his lab. "Hmmm. I've already tried every chemical combination I know of, and yet experiment after experiment results in one failure after another."

Never one to give up, Norton prepared to test the ore running throughout the veins of his newly discovered rock. Approaching the lab table with apprehension mixed with expectation, he carefully scraped away at the embedded substance. His main interest was not in the brown rock itself, but rather its white veins, which felt oily to his touch. Norton surmised that if he could liquefy the oily stuff and add it to the chemicals of his latest experiments, the new white solution might stick to his fur rather than dissolve with the first rain or snowstorm.

Norton began the extraction process by heating the rock until the oil in the veins melted. It took a long time and when the process was finished, only a small amount of thick white goo had been rendered. Norton placed it in a beaker and decided to call it Bleaker Juice. Continuing his scientific thought process, he knew that there wasn't enough Bleaker Juice to experiment separately with each of the three test tubes bubbling in front of him. The question was obvious: which one should he use?

Suddenly, Norton's eyes grew wide and bright. He had a new idea, possibly a breakthrough. "Why not combine the contents of all three tubes into a single beaker? Then I'll add the new substance."

Norton donned his lab coat, gloves, and goggles. Holding his breath, he carefully poured the contents of one tube after another into a new beaker. At first there was much spitting and spewing, as the acids resisted fusion. When the compound was finally achieved, Norton took a deep breath, thankful that the first step was successful. Now for the deciding moment. He poured some of the Bleaker Juice into a bottle topped with a dropper, and carefully squeezed out one drop at a time.

"One, two, three, four..."

The emulsion began to thicken and turn a grayish hue. Suddenly, after the fourth drop was added, a pungent steam began to rise, smoke-like, into the air, emitting a terrible stink. The beaker melted and then shattered, leaving small shards of glass and a pool of oily liquid on the lab table. Finally, to Norton's utter horror, the remaining gaseous substance, hanging like a cloud above the shattered beaker, burst in front of him.

Norton shrieked as the vile mist blew into his face, melting his goggles and exposing his eyes. In an instant, the fur around his eyes, nose, and mouth was singed and smoldering. The mucous membranes of his nose dried up and prickled as if porcupine quills were trapped inside. The penetrating acid in Norton's mouth instantly caused countless oozing cankers. And his eyes, oh his eyes! Even Norton's tears were obliterated.

He had to find a way to wash out the solution even as his anguish continued. Shaking with fear, Norton squeezed his eyes tightly shut and began to grope around, paws seeking the pool of clear water located in the far right corner of his burrow. The basin contained rain water filtering through bedrock, which then seeped through cracks in the burrow wall and trickled down into a natural depression in the burrow's floor.

Not only was Norton blinded, but he was also dizzy and nauseous after the tailspin caused by the explosion. He wasn't even sure which direction to go. Inching forward, Norton bumped into the shelves containing his rock and mineral collections. However, he knew the pool was to the right of the shelves so he slowly began to feel his way in that direction. When he reached the pool, Norton leaned over and was about to scoop up water to flush his sore eyes when he noted its strong smell, something like rotten eggs. To his great misery, Norton realized that the water had been polluted by the aftereffects of the explosion. There was nothing to do but wait and hope that his tears would return, flushing out his sore eyes naturally.

After some time, the stinging pain in Norton's eyes began to subside, only to be replaced by a throbbing headache. Fearful, he opened his eyes. Though barely able to squint, he could distinguish the outlines of his burrow furnishings. The lab, however, was still shrouded by a thick haze. Norton crawled into a corner opposite the polluted pool and as far away from the shattered beaker as possible. The trauma of the event had left him depleted. He curled up into a ball, squeezed his eyes shut, and lapsed into a fitful sleep.

When he awoke, Norton sat upright on his haunches and surveyed the burrow's landscape. Deep in thought, he wondered what had caused the explosion and that terrible stink.

He considered his current predicament. "Still no stripes and now a lab that might be permanently polluted."

But there was something else gnawing at the edge of Norton's mind. As the clouds in his eyes dissipated, he experienced a sudden, clarity of insight and deeper kind of vision. He was struck by a revelation that, for the world of skunks, would prove to be of divine inspiration. He stroked his brow and smiled broadly, realizing that the stink he had stumbled upon could be used as a weapon in the currently weak, skunk-defense arsenal.

"Okay, so maybe I didn't find the stripes I need. But I, Norton Bulymur, have discovered a defense that skunks everywhere can use, a stink bomb of unparalleled potency."

Then another thought nibbled at Norton's consciousness. "Hmmm...what if the compound falls into evil hands? It could be used as a weapon of war and not just for personal protection in the face of danger."

Norton needed to write down the formula and find a secure hiding place.

By the time he ventured out of the burrow, it was dark. Able to see again, Norton peered at the harvest moon and sniffed the acrid air. The eerie, gaseous cloud had wafted out of his burrow and drifted across the land, leaving an oily residue on the plants and forest creatures that had witnessed the explosion. The once fresh air now smelled putrid. Norton began to scavenge along the ground, seeking a hiding place for his secret formula.

"Perhaps I should write the formula on an oak leaf, using the blueberry ink invented by Mordecai. No, that won't work. Once the leaf is old, it will crumble, and the formula will be lost."

Norton spied a cluster of empty acorn shells with fallen caps, leftovers of a squirrel's recent dinner. He grabbed some and brought them back into the lab. After sorting through the pile he chose the largest cap. Using a sharp claw, he scratched the formula into the smooth inner surface of the cap.

Next Norton selected an acorn to match the cap and glued them together with a little tree sap. He scurried back outside where he pulled out a long shoot of ivy crawling on the ground. After removing its leaves, he formed a cord, which he wound tightly around the stem of the cap to create an acorn necklace. After placing the necklace around his neck, Norton left the lab, making a beeline through the woods to Mordecai's burrow in Eastphalia.

As Norton made his way from Westphalia to Eastphalia, he became aware of growing tension in the forest. News of the explosion spread faster than whizzing moles navigating their labyrinths, and the animals were edgy with extra tweets, twitters, thumpings, and a general clamor that increased as he fled. Norton could smell the stench and feel the greasy texture of the underbrush beneath his paws. Travel soon became a slippery business.

Norton was halfway to Eastphalia when he heard the fearsome warning call of the Great Horned Owl, Bubo, dictator of the forest. Norton feared that the pollution caused by the accident in his lab had triggered the inevitable: a frightful forest investigation, conducted by none other than the forest dictator himself. Although Bubo's foreboding hoots and screeches became fainter the farther east Norton traveled, the sinister sounds remained an ominous reminder of Bubo's absolute power. If that wasn't enough to cause worry, there was another matter bothering Norton.

When he arrived in Eastphalia, Norton went directly to his cousin's burrow. Mordecai had been combing out his salt-and-pepper fur, which would not be completely white until the first snowfall. This activity was interrupted when he heard Norton's breathless call at the burrow entrance.

"Mordy where are you? Come quick. I feel faint."

Mordecai dropped his comb and ran to greet Norton, who was shaking from ears to tail and looking dazed. Norton collapsed against Mordecai and was gently led inside after being enfolded by his cousin's protective furry paws.

"What's wrong? Come in, sit down, and tell me all."

Norton's words came in a gasping rush. "I... have... something... to show you." With paws quivering, Norton removed the crude necklace from around his neck and carefully unglued the acorn's cap, revealing to Mordecai the secret formula scratched within its smooth inner wall.

In hushed tones, Norton explained the details of his discovery. "Mordy, my explosion polluted the forest. I'm certain Bubo will convene a Critter Congress, and that can only mean one thing: trouble for the skunks. And there's something else. My secret concoction is useless without a delivery system. You are the only one who can invent just the right kind of contraption, my best friend and clever cousin."

~ 2 ~

The Skunks Are Banished

It was always the Great Horned Owl, ruler of the forest, who convened a meeting whenever something of magnitude occurred in the forests of Eastphalia or Westphalia. This assemblage, consisting of one member from each animal family, and known as the Critter Congress, took place at a designated spot midway between Eastphalia and Westphalia. From as far back as the beginning of the forests, the designation of Ruler was given to the oldest member of the Bubo family because of their great vision, genius, and wisdom.

However, the Bubo of these times had neither genius nor wisdom. This Bubo was a jealous bird with a mean streak. He had stolen the title of Ruler from his weak uncle by forcing him to abdicate shortly before his untimely death. Although it couldn't be proven, there was gossip among the animal families that Bubo had advanced his uncle's demise by poisoning him.

The forest animals were so afraid of Bubo they sought refuge whenever the shadow of his menacing wings crossed the sky at dusk. Thus, when the meltdown in Norton Bulymur's laboratory occurred, the responsibility of convening the Critter Congress was upon the wings of this mean and hateful Bubo. Flying across the early evening sky, he alerted the Congressional Designees.

Critter Congresses were always large because of the many different species living in the forest, and this one was no exception, soon growing to epic proportions. Animals not ordinarily seen together were huddled closely. A beaver, hearing Bubo's call, quickly left his den in one of the many woodland streams. His wet fur twitched as he stood next to a brown wolf with darting eyes, drooling mouth, and large teeth. In front of the wolf was a fearful opossum, playing dead despite the purpose of the occasion. A porcupine with sharp quills in defensive mode stood next to a gray wolf, who had his eye on a large rabbit.

In a sudden display of attention—forgetting their natural instincts—the Critter Congress noted Bubo's arrival. Bubo perched on his favorite limb and readied himself to address the nervous assembly. The animals, all ears, were anxious to hear the message, knowing it would be revolutionary. Bubo cleared his throat and puffed out his feathered chest before speaking.

"My fellow furred and feathered families, I called you here today to discuss an event that caused the recent pollution in our forest. We all know that Norton Bulymer has been experimenting with chemicals for years, trying to find a solution to his personal deformity. Unfortunately, this time he went too far. Not only did he pollute the forest but he may have stumbled upon a discovery, one which he and his kind could misuse. The consequences would be calamitous."

A general rumbling broke out among the Critter Congress representatives. Then one of the animals raised its paw.

"I see there is a question from the back of the gathering," said Bubo. "What is it? Speak up and be brief, for there is much to accomplish this evening."

A stammering voice asked, "What is this discovery you think Norton and the skunks could misuse?"

"Ah, yes... about the discovery. In my wisdom—I *am* head of the forest for a reason—I surmised that the solution Norton discovered, the very one that polluted our pristine forest, could be used as a weapon against skunk predators, causing an imbalance in the forest's natural equilibrium. Second, as a member of the Mephitist genus within the Mephitidae family, Norton would undoubtedly share this newfound formula with the other skunk types, including the Spilogales, the Conepatuses and the Mydauses. Third and worst of all is that the skunks would have access to a weapon of mass destruction, not to mention the potential permanent pollution of the forests. I'm afraid that Norton and *all* skunks must be banished forever."

Bubo's large yellow glowing eyes, fixated on the gathering as he silently swiveled his head from right to left and then left to right moving a full 180 degrees in each direction.

"Do I hear a motion to banish Norton and the skunks? If there isn't any discussion, I will make such a motion, and I further feel that we must gather a search party immediately."

The silence in the forest, brought on by Bubo's words, was broken by Mephuselah Mink, eldest of the Mephitidae and the family's Congressional Representative. Mephuselah became defensive, vociferously expressing his displeasure regarding Bubo's accusations. Mephuselah's voice, although warbled by age, was nonetheless animated.

"How dare you…you…autocrat. We Mephitidae have never been able to defend ourselves very well. Norton's discovery could help curb the appetites of all you fat owls."

Bubo, who had never been challenged, was infuriated by Mephuselah's insult. He flattened the feathered tufts on either side of his ears and swooped from his perch toward the old mink, emitting a loud screech. Mephuselah saw his enemy fast approaching and escaped into the woods, heading straight to his inventive grand-cousin, Mordecai. He was certain to find Norton there, and they both needed to be warned.

~ 3 ~

Mordecai's Invention

Mordecai stroked his whiskers, a thoughtful expression on his face as he pondered the dual challenges of the dilemma. First, Norton needed an apparatus that could effectively deliver the new chemical compound. Second, where or how could it be concealed? Mordecai used a simple slab of wood positioned on top of four short logs as his worktable. A large sheet of birch bark was stretched on the tabletop alongside a cup of mashed blueberries mixed with mud. This he used to draft blueprints of his many inventions. After a few minutes of deliberation, Mordecai dipped one of his claws into the inky mixture, and with a few quick strokes a blueprint began to take form.

As he sketched, Mordecai explained his contraption idea to Norton. "It will be a gadget with two settings: one that delivers a stream, and one that delivers a spray."

When he finished, the drawing looked something like a modern squirt gun. An adjustable nozzle at the top was attached to a narrow tube that went into a container holding the solution. The nozzle could be rotated, allowing discharge of the liquid in either a spray or a stream.

Mordecai continued, "The container needs to be small so it can be easily hidden under...hmmm, under your tail. Yes, your tail would be the perfect hiding place, and I think I can make the pump action strong enough so that you'll be able to shoot up to a distance of fifteen feet."

Norton stared at the blueprint, in awe of his cousin's remarkable idea. "But Mordy, how will it attach under my tail?"

"Hmmm, let me think about that one."

* * *

After traveling half the night, the old mink finally arrived in Eastphalia and went directly to Mordecai's burrow. Moving down the entry tunnel, Mephuselah heard his grandnephews engaged in animated conversation. He announced his presence with a loud, "Ahem."

Norton and Mordecai looked up, startled. Composing himself, Mordecai invited his aged grand-cousin in for a cup of very strong tea, which had been brewing all night. While ushering Mephuselah to the table, Mordecai furtively waved his right paw and motioned for Norton to cover the worktable with a nearby cloth, hoping to conceal the blueprint. After an awkward pause, the three settled around the table for tea.

Mephuselah recounted the evening's recent events, including what Bubo had said during the Critter Congress as well as Bubo's attack. Finally Mephuselah said in a quavering voice, "All skunks are in grave danger. Norton, your only recourse is to flee forever."

Norton's whiskers began to twitch and Mordecai's tail began to stiffen. Their nervousness intensified when they realized that steam from the teapot was causing a damp spot on the tablecloth. As their eyes darted in alarm, the blueprint, which was bleeding through the cloth, became a visible copy of the spray apparatus.

Mephuselah immediately understood the purpose of the invention he could now clearly see, the very type of invention that had caused Bubo's reaction.

"Mordecai, your apparatus is clever. I can envision uses for it in the future, but there isn't enough time to build it now. You need to gather as many skunks as possible and escape. Bubo's words have caused a stir and our enemies are gathering a hunting party as we speak. It's time to hightail it out of here."

As Mephuselah pushed himself away from the table, he emitted a short blast from his hind end. "Please excuse my tail toot. The tea must have been too strong."

Mordecai excused his elderly cousin and thanked him for the warning. "We'll contact you once we formulate an escape plan."

"Don't take too long. I'll be waiting to hear from you."

After Mephuselah left, Norton turned to Mordecai. "Look Mordy, Mephuselah gave me an idea, but first let's get back to my lab."

So while most of the forest was asleep, Norton and Mordecai hastened from Eastphalia to Westphalia.

Once at the lab, Norton explained his idea. "When Mephuselah accidentally had a tail toot, it made me think about what causes tail toots."

"Yeah? So what does that have to do with your situation?"

"Mordy, just listen. There's no time to think up another type of contraption much less how I would fasten it under my tail. So, it's obvious...I'll just swallow the solution. Then, with a simple tail toot, as Mephuselah so titled it, I'll emit the a vile vapor as a defense mechanism."

Norton glanced at a horrified Mordecai and walked rapidly to the lab table where a pool of the spilled liquid remained. Before Mordecai could intervene, Norton lapped it up.

Within minutes, Norton's stomach became distended, his tail shot straight up, and he excused himself from the lab. As he left, with a wry smile on his face he said, "The heck with Mephuselah's tail toots. A fart is a fart is a fart, and it isn't going to smell like a rose. I'll be back later."

With that, Norton left a flabbergasted Mordecai staring after him.

Norton was deep into the forest when he spied a farmhouse in the distance. It was the perfect place to "toot and scoot," since he didn't want to further alarm the forest families. He suspected that this was the Hubbard House since the Hubbard's had inhabited that part of the woods for as long as

Norton could remember. Once inside, he let the fermented gases rip, breaking the wind with the first of his silent, but deadly, farts.

After relieving himself of the first phase of gas, Norton heard a hubbub taking place in the room next to the now polluted parlor. He crept into the kitchen and away from the parlor, which now smelled like a mixture of rotten eggs, garlic, and burnt rubber. Norton watched three mice running around an old woman, who was most likely the mother of the abode. She was brandishing a carving knife and chasing the mice away from a large wheel of Muenster cheese. All at once she gave a whack with her knife, wounding the tail of one of the mice.

Norton became nervous and could not control his next fart. With a loud, spppplaaaat, he unintentionally discharged a noisy, smelly one in the direction of the three mice, who were immediately blinded. Mother Hubbard, holding her nose, ran out of the house, fleeing the foul odor that now permeated her home. Inside, the three blind mice scampered aimlessly in all directions, bumping into each other as well as the kitchen furniture. Norton realized what had happened, given his own recent, loss of vision, and felt remorseful for temporarily blinding the small innocent critters.

Spying the cheese on the larder's bottom shelf, Norton crept toward it, not wanting to frighten the mice with his presence, and reaching up, was able to pull it down, dragging the wheel of Muenster to the center of the room where the mice were now huddled.

The largest mouse, almost the size of a rat, called out in a squeaky voice, "Who goes there?"

Norton answered, "Nobody."

"Then nobody has blinded me and my two friends," the rat-sized mouse said.

The mice began to nibble the cheese, except for the smallest one. It seemed disinterested in the cheese, preferring to get as far from the house as possible. So when Norton fled the scene heading back to his lab, the little mouse, using its keen sense of smell, tailed him.

~ 4 ~

The Escape Plan

After Mordecai recovered from the shock brought on by Norton's recklessness, he began to pace, deep in thought with brow furrowed and paws clasped tightly behind him. As he paced, he pondered Mephuselah's parting words: It's time to hightail it out of here. Still pacing, Mordecai began to whisper under his whiskers.

"So, the problem is…the skunks need to escape. But how? They can't run away. With Bubo's night vision and his ability to fly, he'll have no problem locating the skunks and relaying the information to the hunting party. Maybe they could go underground. But no, that would only be a temporary measure. Eating worms and grubs as a steady diet would be unacceptable. Maybe they could swim away. Yes…escape by water. That's the only answer. Hmmm, that won't work either. Skunks can't swim distances, and these skunks need to go *far* away."

Scratching his head with the sharpest of his claws, Mordecai continued ruminating. "What'll I do? I'm supposed to be the inventive one. So far, it's been Norty, not me, who's come up with all the bright ideas. All I've done is invent some futuristic gadget and tell him to hide the formula under his tail. What good is that? The least I can do now is figure out an escape plan. I can't let him down again."

Mordecai felt overwhelmed. He needed time to think so he crawled under the lab table, seeking a place where he could dwell on the problem. But it was no use. He was exhausted, and soon curled up and went to sleep. While napping, he had an inspirational dream about his favorite Aunt Agram, who had recently died.

Upon waking, Mordecai knew exactly how to solve the problem. He crawled out from under the table in great excitement. "Wait I've got an idea. Why didn't I think of it before now? Thank you. Thank you, Auntie."

In the past, whenever he needed inspiration, Mordecai employed a problem solving technique called auntagramming, which he named after his dear Aunt Agram. She would select one of the words spoken in the last phrase or sentence of a conversation related to the particular issue at hand. Next she would rearrange the letters of the selected word until an answer to the predicament was revealed.

Rushing outside, Mordecai headed for a group of birch trees behind the lab. He stripped off several sheets of tree bark and hurried back. Staring at the first of the blank sheets, he pondered.

"What was the last thing Norton said before ingesting the solution?" He tried to remember the conversation. "Norton said something about farts. Let me see. Did he say, 'A fart smells.'? No, there was more to it than that. He mentioned a rose, too. I think he might have said, 'A fart can't smell like a rose.' Wait a minute, he said fart more than once. 'A fart is a fart is a fart and…it isn't going to smell like a rose.' Yes, that was it. Then he said he would be right back. So all together Norton's last words were, 'A fart is a fart is a fart, and it isn't going to smell like a rose. I'll be right back.' Yes, now I'm sure. Those were Norty's exact words before bolting."

Mordecai paced around the worktable. "Which of the words should I select? The very last word Norton said was 'back.' So I'll try that one first."

He dipped a claw into some of the blueberry mud ink and wrote B-A-C-K in large letters on the sheet of birch bark. Then Mordecai began the rearranging process. First A-C-K-B, then C-A-B-K, followed by K-A-C-B.

"No, nothing there." Mordecai continued his thought process, "Well, how about 'rose'? I once knew a Rose, she was beautiful. But oh my, those thorns."

Mordecai again dipped one claw into the blueberry ink and wrote R-O-S-E in large letters on a sheet of birch bark. Once again he began to rearrange the letters. First he tried O-R-S-E, then E-S-R-O, and lastly S-O-R-E. Mordecai's eyes glazed over as his attention was interrupted by thoughts of Rose and her hurtful thorns.

Then he said, "Yup, her thorns did leave me sore, but nope, wrong topic and definitely not the right point."

Again Mordecai thought about Norton's last words, repeating them slowly, "A fart is a fart is a fart, and it isn't going to smell like a rose." Mordecai shouted, "Fart! The word must be 'fart,' since Norton said it three times."

For the third time, Mordecai eagerly dipped a claw into the ink, and wrote F-A-R-T in extra-large letters. He rapidly began the rearrangement. T-R-A-F... F-R-A-T... T-A-R-F, and finally, R-A-F-T.

"Oh my stars! For the love of the sun and the moon. That's it!" Mordecai began to dance about, shouting, "Raft. Raft. Raft. We need to build a raft."

Mordecai spent the rest of the night creating blueprints of his envisioned raft including separate spaces for kitchen and workrooms. At dawn he stretched, peered down at his work, and wiped his brow. "Whew, I'm finally finished. The blueprints are perfect. What a surprise I'll have for Norty when he gets back."

Sitting back, Mordecai contemplated his work and began reviewing each blueprint until he realized something was wrong.

"They're beautiful, but... oh, great. Brilliant. I've done it again. Another impossible, foolish idea. The skunks can't be transported by design alone. They need a real raft. Now just how is that supposed to happen?"

Distraught, Mordecai left the lab. He wandered about the woods until, by chance, he arrived at the river bank. For a while he simply gazed out at the blackness of the river below, self-absorbed and thoughtful. He was feeling distinctly hopeless when a noisy buzzing followed by a loud crash jolted him out of his doldrums. Just as Mordecai turned to see what the commotion was, a large tree crashed down so close he could feel the earth tremble. Immediately he knew the cause of the racket.

"It's the beavers. They're all over the place, building their dams and lodges. Of course! That's it! It's so obvious. They're the best builders around these parts. If they can build dams and lodges, why not a raft? I need to get down to the river."

Mordecai scurried down the bank, determined to talk the beavers into building a raft according to his blueprints.

Standing straight and tall, he stretched himself up to look important, put a convincing smile on his weaselly face, and strutted over to the hardiest looking beaver.

"Hi. Let me introduce myself. I'm Mordecai Wilhelm of the Weasel Family, and I'm looking for who's in charge."

"Well, that would be me," the hardy-looking beaver said. "Name's Brenston and I'm the head honcho of this here crew. What can I do for ya?"

"I've been admiring your fine workmanship," said Mordecai, "and it looks like you're almost finished."

"Yeah, just about."

"Then I guess you'll be on to your next venture soon, correct?"

"Well, we don't have anything planned right now, but as ya know, we beavers like to keep busy."

"Say, my cousin and I are in a bit of a bind, and I was wondering if I might interest you in a little proposition that could be beneficial to us both."

"Maybe I would, and maybe I wouldn't. So tell me, pal, whatcha got in mind?"

"Have you ever heard of a skunk named Norton Bulymur?"

"Yeah, ya mean that oddball chemist...lives near here?"

"Yes, exactly. That's him. He's in trouble with Bubo, that miserable, so-called Ruler of the forest. There was a big meeting and—"

"Yeah, we heard all about it through the mill."

"The mill?"

"Aw come on. You know: the rumor mill."

"Right. Well, so here's the problem, Brenston. Bubo banished all the skunks from the forest, and he's organizing a search party."

"Sounds like something Bubo would do."

"By the way, not only is Norton my cousin, he's also my best friend. I fear for him and the safety of all the skunks. You know how brutal Bubo is."

"Yeah, but we don't pay attention to no big bird. In case ya didn't know, we river animals run our own show down here. And we don't take orders from some screechy owl. Fact is, he's had it in for us for a long time now, 'cause we never go to his meetings, and we don't pay no attention to his commands."

"Well, then, let me just say this. While the skunks are the first of the animals to be banished, I don't think Bubo will stop there. His vengeful ways are a danger to us all," Mordecai said.

"So what ya got planned?"

"I'm an inventor and have designed a getaway raft for the skunks. Norton is an explorer as well as a chemist and has told me he's heard tell of beautiful lush forests that lie on the other side of the great waters. Problem is, although I'm an inventor, I'm not a builder. The skunks need a strong raft capable of transporting them a great distance to a new land."

"So that's where we come in, yeah?"

"You bet. Nobody's better with wood than the beavers."

"You might not be no builder, but I gotta say you hammered the nail on the head with that one." Brenston puffed up with pride. "Why, we can build you the strongest raft you ever seen."

"Then you'll help us?"

"Why not? It's a change from our usual work, but as I see it... a job's a job. Might as well be working for you. Besides, all we ever build is dams and lodges, lodges and dams. This here raft thing might be fun and besides, it don't hurt to stick it to that old owl."

While Mordecai was making his deal with Brenston, Norton was leaving the farmhouse and farts far behind, making his way back to Westphalia. Norton knew Bubo was organizing a search party, and his fear escalated as he traveled. Every time there was even the slightest clearing in the trees, he imagined the broad, shadowed wings of Bubo soaring overhead.

Norton was sure he was being followed, and that wasn't his only concern. He fretted over the ill he had caused the mice as well as the potency of the gas. He really needed guidance on the use and control of his discovered chemical solution.

By the time Norton rounded the last bend before coming home to his lab, he had worked himself into a frenzy of fear and guilt. Exhausted, he tripped and slumped down. Mordecai, who had been reviewing the beaver's work while on the lookout for Norton, saw him stumble. Immediately Mordecai rushed up the hillside. Breathless, he ran over to Norton in great excitement.

"Thank heavens you're here, Norton. You look frightful... are you all right? I was quite worried after you left." Taking a deep breath Mordecai said, "Please tell me what happened."

Norton wearily recited the events, pouring out his guilt and sadness for blinding the three mice in the Hubbard house. Then he lowered his voice and leaned toward Mordecai. "I think Bubo might be following me." He continued with his worst fears. "Mordy, this is mighty strong stuff and must be used only when a nonnegotiable defense is needed. It's critical that the solution be used in a responsible manner. I need to find a way to control this substance."

"Never mind that right now. You and the other skunks need to get to get out of here."

"I know, but how?"

"Glad you asked. I've been working on an escape plan. If you're strong enough to come down to the river I'll explain."

"I'm much better now that I'm home, so let's go."

Norton accompanied Mordecai and watched in awe at the speed and power of the beavers sawing down trees and yelling, "Timber!" The neatly stacked logs looked very much like a small lumber yard.

"Mordy, what's all this beaver business about?" Norton asked in bewilderment.

Mordecai explained how he used Aunt Agram's technique to come up with the idea for a raft. "I've employed the beavers to build a raft large enough to take you and the rest of the skunks away from here."

"That's an unbelievable plan but I'm not surprised, my clever cousin. Only you could have thought this up."

"Well, I did have a little help from my aunt. Listen, Norty. I think we've both had enough for now. It's almost sunrise. Let's try to get some rest. We'll talk more tomorrow."

The two settled in and slept for the day.

Upon waking, Norton stretched, rubbed his eyes, and sighed. "Mordy, it feels good to finally have a decent day's rest."

"You said it, but now we must hurry. Do you know what direction to go once you begin your journey?"

"Don't worry. I know how to chart our voyage and can plan the best escape route. The river leads out to a larger body of water, which dumps into an even larger body of water and then, hopefully, to a new land. And salvation for the skunks."

The cousins spent much of that night deliberating over a myriad of details regarding the raft. Discussion turned from the size and shape of the raft to the tasks needed to accomplish the mission. Just before dawn, Mordecai announced, "I shall dub you Captain, and henceforth you shall be known as

Norton Bulymur, Captain of the Skunk Salvation Seekers."

Norton, who was very touched by the appointment made by his beloved cousin, suddenly felt an overwhelming sadness.

"But, what about you, Mordy, I can't imagine a life without you, we are the Norty and Mordy Team."

Mordecai's feelings mirrored Norton's. "I, too, cannot imagine a life without you, Norty."

"Then join me as first mate." Norton cried.

Mordecai stood on his hind legs and proclaimed, "Be it known to all, near and far, that Norton Bulymur, Captain of the Skunk Salvation Seekers, has, without further ado, appointed Mordecai Wilhelm to the position of first mate."

Exhausted from recent events, they ate, drank, and fell into a deep slumber just before the dawn of a new day cracked the horizon. The two didn't awaken until the next night, shortly after moonrise.

"Norty, Norty, wake up. Come on, we overslept. You need to fetch Mephuselah back in Eastphalia. You're supposed to tell him our escape plan. And I need to get down to the river and check on the beavers."

Norton stirred slowly. Then, realizing he and the skunks had little time left for their escape, he shook his shiny fur to speed the awakening process.

"Consider me on my way. See you later, Mordy."

Norton scampered out of the lab heading east, while Mordecai rushed to the river. When Mordecai reached a spot along the cliff where the trees thinned, he skidded to a halt and gazed at the miracle below. In front of his disbelieving eyes was an almost complete raft.

The beavers had built the main platform by adjoining long logs, with additional logs placed crosswise underneath to give the vessel support and buoyancy. They bound the logs together with reeds harvested from the long, sturdy grasses growing along the river bank. For cement they used the sticky muck that oozed up from the river bed. The biggest surprise was the raft's two triangular, white sails that were billowing in the breeze.

Mordecai was astonished. Not only had the beavers built a magnificent raft, but the addition of sails completely bowled him over. Sails were not in his original plans. Where had they come from?

Mordecai began to holler, "Brenston...Brenston. Hello there..."

Brenston began to look around. "Where you at?"

"Up here. I'm up on top."

"Hold on, I'm coming."

Brenston lumbered up the riverbank, hampered by his tail, which was extra large, very flat, and oar-like, dragging from his behind.

Mordecai saw how difficult it was for Brenston and began to scamper down. "Wait, I'll come down and meet you."

As he raced downhill, Mordecai gathered speed, heading straight toward the beaver. The two would have collided had Mordecai not been able to skid to a stop directly in front of his new friend. Both were out of breath and panting, but Mordecai couldn't contain his excitement about the raft and his curiosity about the mysterious sails.

"How in the name of the sun and the moon and the stars did you accomplish so much so fast?"

"Oh, it was nothing. Us beavers are fast workers. Besides, me and the crew, well…we wanna help the skunks. Plus, it was even funner than I expected."

"This craft is much finer than I ever imagined… why, it certainly is a seaworthy vessel. I have only one question."

"Well, what is it? What do you wanna know?"

"The raft has sails. How did that happen? They weren't in my blueprints. Who came up with the idea? How were they made?"

"Uh…thought ya had one question. I count three. Come on. Let's get over to the raft. We can talk on the way. See, it's kind of a long story."

So Mordecai followed a slow-going Brenston, who shuffled over to the water's edge where they could better see the raft, already afloat in the water.

"See, here's what happened. I was doin' my job, supervising my workers, when Beats—boy, he's really something, cutting down trees faster than any of them other beavers, using some kind of pattern when he saws. Anyway Beats comes over to me and says he seen two spiders on one of the logs. Thinks they're poisonous and shouldn't be used for the raft. So I tell him 'I'll have a look.' Ya know, it's hard work cutting down all them trees and I'm not getting rid of a log unless I have to. So I go over and check it out and, yup, two black spiders, hanging upside down in one of them knot holes. It was weird because their bellies were pink instead of red. So I say to them, real nice-like, 'Excuse me, I hope you mean me no harm, just passing through.

I'm not looking to cause no trouble here.' Then they tell me not to worry 'cuz they couldn't hurt a fly even if they wanted to. Said they're too depressed. So I ask them, 'What are yous depressed about?' They tell me they shouldn't be talking to me 'cause we're strangers. So I tell them my name, and they tell me theirs, and that sorta eases 'em into talking a little more."

"Interesting story, Brenston. What *are* their names?"

"Sis and Sass, and they're twin sisters."

"Okay, but that still doesn't explain the sails."

"Hold on, I'm getting to that part. Sis, she's the older one, starts telling me why she's depressed, but Sass pert' near tells her to shut up about it. Says it makes her feel guilty. Then Sis tells Sass to mind her own business and starts spilling the beans. She tells me both their mates died in some kinda accident and now they're widows. Then when I asked them how their old men kicked the bucket, Sass got real mad and yelled at Sis, saying 'I warned you not to say too much.' I thought maybe their old men got ate by worms. When I said that, they both started crying real hard, and even Sis said it was too terrible to talk about—"

"Look, I get it," Mordecai interrupted. "Twin black widow spiders lost their mates and are depressed. That explains a lot about the spiders, but not about how the raft came to have sails."

"I told ya it's a long story."

Mordecai sighed. "Sorry, Brenston, just tell me the rest."

"Okay, okay. I'll get to the point 'cuz I can see you're kinda in a hurry to know about them sails."

"Well, yes, that was my original question."

"So I tell the sisters they should go along for the ride with you and the skunks. I tell 'em it would be like starting over. Way better than moping around here. Like a vacation, with sea air and sunshine. So Sass says to Sis, 'Hmmm.' And that's when I knew I had 'em. Ya see, spiders love to spin webs and with them on board, I figure they could spin up some big webs to use as sails. When the wind hits those sails, wow! So does that answer your question?"

"Genius, Brenston, sheer genius."

~ 5 ~

Mephuselah's Gathering

While Mordecai was checking on the beaver's progress Norton found his grand-cousin Mephuselah snoozing on a bed of scented needles under one of the pine trees that grew behind his burrow. Gently, Norton shook him.

"Wake up. It's me, Norton."

Mephuselah was dreaming and difficult to rouse. Again Norton shook him, this time more forcefully, and spoke directly into his ear. "Grand-cousin Mephuselah, it's Norton. Wake up. Wake up! Mordy and I have an escape plan."

Mephuselah rubbed his eyes, shook his head, and then recognizing Norton said, "Escape plan? Oh, oh yes, now I remember."

After he was fully awake, Mephuselah and Norton retreated into the burrow to discuss the plan.

"Grand-cousin, Mordecai used Aunt Agram's thinking process to figure out a means of escape. He came up with the brilliant idea of building a raft! Not only that, he convinced a den of beavers to build the raft for us."

"Why, that's remarkable. Now tell me, I'm curious. What word did Mordecai unscramble to come up with the idea of a raft?"

"Well, you won't like this, but he used the word *fart*."

"In heaven's name, how did he ever come up with that word, of all words?"

"Remember before you left Mordecai's burrow, you made what you called a tail toot? Well..."

All Mephuselah could say was, "Phew."

"Listen," continued Norton, "Mordy appointed me Captain of The Skunk Salvation Seekers."

"Skunk Salvation Seekers...I like it."

"There's something else...Mordecai decided to join the Seekers, and I appointed him first mate."

"I'm not surprised. You two have been inseparable since you were small kits. Now how can I help?"

"Mordy and I want you to round up as many skunks as you can to join us."

"Norton, leave it to me. I'll contact the skunk families. There won't be room for all the skunks in the forest, but we should send as many kits as possible, of those who have reached their Enlightenment year. The family elders can bring the selected kits here, where I'll prep them for the journey. Then I'll lead them to you and Mordecai back in Westphalia."

Norton felt relieved that these matters would be handled by Mephuselah, and after saying goodbye, he sped back to Westphalia.

Mephuselah made haste contacting each of the families, who quickly organized their skunk kits and brought them to his burrow. As each family arrived, he greeted and then interviewed the kits and their parents, sorting out the strongest to join the Salvation Seekers.

The skunk families knew there was a high probability of extinction unless Norton's newfound defense mechanism could be further developed, it was agreed among them to allow their kits to band together and join Captain Norton Bulymur and First Mate Mordecai Wilhelm in their escape from the forests of Eastphalia and Westphalia.

Since Mephuselah wanted to find a suitable mate for Norton, he paid extra attention to the female kits. None impressed him until the arrival of a family whose burrow was far away. As the parents escorted their only kit, Celeste, to Mephuselah, he was stunned by her beauty. Her eyes were bright and sparkly, ears perky, and whiskers silky, with two shiny white stripes forming a perfect V-shape against the soft fur of her back. However, it was her tail that caught Mephuselah's eye. It was large and bushy, and she carried it high in the air with pride, swishing it from side to side as she walked. She was, to Mephuselah's mind, the perfect mate for Norton.

Celeste was hesitant about leaving her parents, the den of her birth, and her familiar woodlands, especially for an adventure that would take her into uncharted waters. Her Year of Pretendment would soon be over, and she would enter the Year of Enlightenment before the next moon. Her parents knew that uniting their offspring with Norton Bulymur—now the most famous of all forest skunks—would be an excellent match. Even though Norton remained stripeless, he was after all, now a captain, and the very title carried its own mark of distinction.

Mephuselah gathered the troupe of select skunk kits along with their parents and led them to a secret gathering place in the middle of the woodlands. It was a clearing not far from the old Hubbard House, but a good distance from the site of the Critter Congress. It was there that the kits would separate from their parents and follow Mephuselah to Westphalia, where the departure point was being readied.

* * *

Norton and Mordecai reunited in Westphalia and embraced one another in a brotherly hug. The cousins were so excited and in such a hurry to impart their separate pieces of information that they both began speaking in a jumble of simultaneous chatter.

"I can't wait 'til you see the raft..."

"Cousin Mephuselah is going to..."

"It even has sails and there are..."

The piecemeal chitchat went on and on, until the excitement left them out of breath.

Finally, Mordecai said, "Just follow me down to the riverbank. You won't believe your eyes."

During the trek, they were able to discuss what happened while they were apart. At the riverbank, Mordecai stretched out his paws in a triumphant gesture as he displayed the now finished raft. It was complete with two billowing silk sails, topped off by the twin, black, widowed spiders at the tops of the masts, with their showy underbellies, now red again, as constant warning signals.

A crew of beavers in assigned positions aboard the raft practiced paddling motions. Ten beavers faced each other on each of the long sides of the raft. Their plump behinds and flat tails were immersed in the river, where they scooped up the water with their oar-like tails. Along with the twenty beavers on the long sides, there was one beaver on each of the two short sides. The two beavers at either end established the front and back of the rectangular raft.

Brenston, the largest of the crew members and previously the raft's building project supervisor, was so enraptured with the skunk cause that he had agreed to assist Norton and Mordecai in their quest for salvation. It was he who convinced the rest of the beaver builders to do the same. Despite his sensitive nature, Brenston was quite stern during work hours and a natural leader, able to properly steer the beaver workers. For this reason, Norton selected him to be in charge of steering, which took place at the back of the raft.

At the other end of the raft was Beatoven Beaver, known to all for his rhythmic sawing abilities. Because of this skill, he was chosen to synchronize the beavers' rowing rhythms. Beatoven used a tree bough to conduct the beavers. So with Brenston steering in the back, or stern, of the raft and Beatoven conducting in the front, or bow, the raft's rowing rhythm was established.

Sis and Sass sat atop their billowing sails. Sis, the older and bossier of the sisters, insisted on creating the mainsail. And as the mainsail, she refused to go up and down the pole, preferring to hang upside down on top of her mast as a permanent lookout. Sass, who tended to be argumentative, only agreed to spin her silk after she was titled headsail. As headsail, it would be her responsibility to catch the wind by bringing her sail up and down the pole as directed by Brenston. After that, she too would hang upside down on top of her mast as an additional lookout along with her sister.

So Captain Norton, First Mate Mordecai, Sis, Sass, Brenston, Beatoven, twenty rowing beavers, and the skunk kits would comprise the raft's occupants...with additional room for the inevitable offspring, should their voyage be a long one. Unbeknownst to them, the small mouse that had been following Norton ever since he polluted the Hubbard House, sneaked on board as a stowaway, hiding near the kitchen where it would be able to pilfer food and water.

* * *

Back in the clearing in Eastphalia, the skunk kits and their parents huddled together for protection against the openness of the space. They listened intently to Mephuselah's warbling words as he briefed his flock:

"Dear ones, the skunks have reached a crossroads, and so it is, with a heavy heart, that we must say goodbye to the kits standing before us. As the eldest of the family members, I speak for all the remaining forest skunks who have asked me to send their fond farewells and genuine blessings. The great responsibility to forge new paths and seek the freedom needed for the future of Skunkdom now belongs to you. I have selected equal numbers of males and females from each of the skunk families and grant you the power to populate unknown frontiers, develop new skills, and defend yourselves in the face of danger. It will be up to you and your offspring to determine what evils may lurk in the new land and when to use this ultimate new weapon discovered by your captain, Norton Bulymur. You must remain true to skunk natures, true to your surroundings, and deal equitably with other animals you meet in your travels. May the moon and the stars guide you by night and the sun by day; may the winds, the waters, and all your encounters assist you on your passage; and may you safely reach the destination for which you are fated."

With his statement about the moon and stars, Mephuselah directed the flock to look up into the night sky. There were collective oohs and ahhs, since none but Mephuselah had ever seen the moon or stars due to the great density of the trees in the forest. A hush descended as Mephuselah began to speak again.

"The stars and moon have secret stories to tell. They will be a constant source of evening entertainment for you throughout your journey, as will the sun and clouds during the day. Heed the wonderment around you, show respect for the resources you discover, and be fruitful and multiply."

At the conclusion of his speech, Mephuselah directed the separation of the kits from their tearful parents. Lining up in order from smallest to largest, the kits followed Mephuselah into the forest. He guided them through the night toward Westphalia and adventures they could never have imagined.

~ 6 ~

All Aboard

Mephuselah and his select group of Skunk Salvation Seekers rounded the last bend to the riverbank. A welcome fanfare greeted them, organized by Captain Norton Bulymur and First Mate Mordecai Wilhelm, with preparations made by the crew. The beavers, thumping their tails against the side of the raft in a royal greeting, were led by Beatoven Beaver waving his conducting bough. No longer able to contain themselves, the kits dashed forward, all except young Celeste who preferred to remain with Mephuselah. Although he could still scurry, Mephuselah's dashing days were over.

Captain Norton Bulymur and First Mate Mordecai Wilhelm stood in front of the raft, ready to bestow official greetings and introductions once all had arrived. It only took a few extra minutes for Mephuselah and Celeste to join the crowd. As they came down the leaf-strewn path, the moon—which was winking through some stubborn leaves still holding on to their branches—lit up the perfect white V-shaped stripes on Celeste's shiny back. Norton, who until that moment had no interest in the females of his species, was thunderstruck by Celeste's beauty. Celeste shyly met Norton's gaze. The connection was made, the looks unmistakable. It was love at first sight.

After making merry until dawn, all were tired from the festivities and settled down to sleep. That evening, Norton and Mordecai were awake at dusk, just in time to see a large, magenta sun melt into the river, streaking the sky above and the water below with shades of pink and aquamarine. The sky and the water deepened into navy blue within the hour.

Mephuselah joined Norton and Mordecai, and the three began to rouse the kits and the beavers, as well as Sis and Sass who were snoozing on top of their masts.

Captain Norton shouted, "All aboard who's coming aboard."

First Mate Mordecai assisted the animals onto the waiting raft. With sleepy eyelids still heavy, they boarded, joining Sis, Sass, and unknown to them, the stowaway mouse.

Finally, only Norton, Mordecai, and Mephuselah remained ashore, saying their farewells. Mephuselah, who understood that rigorous travel at his age would be precarious, declined the offer to join the Skunk Salvation Seekers' quest.

As they stood at the shore, Mephuselah told Mordecai how impressed he was with the design and construction of the raft. Then he said, "We need a fitting name for this raft of yours which, by the way, looks more like a barge."

Norton and Wilhelm had been too busy to think of naming the craft, but agreed with the old mink.

Norton said, "Mephuselah, if it hadn't been for your guidance, we would never have reached this day. So I wish to bestow upon you the honor of naming our sturdy vessel, or barge as you have so astutely called it."

"Hmmm. Well, let me see," said Mephuselah, who welcomed both the tribute and the responsibility. "I know! We should name it after you, Norton. If it hadn't been for your discovery, well, you know the rest. It shall be known as...I've got it...yes, the Norton Bulymur Captain Barge."

Then Mordecai said,

"I agree but don't you think the name is a bit too long?"

Mephuselah paused, stroking his whiskers. "We can shorten it by using initials. How about the NBC Barge?"

In unison, the cousins expressed their approval. Mephuselah wished them good speed and then with parting words he said, "Follow your hopes, dreams, aspirations and the stars, as well as yourselves, to chart your way."

With that, Norton and Mordecai boarded the NBC Barge. Mephuselah gave a shove, Beatoven tapped out the rowing rhythm, Sis and Sass adjusted the sails, and they were off, departing the lands of Eastphalia and Westphalia forever.

Captain Norton Bulymur chose to follow the river along its natural course until the NBC Barge reached the rumored larger bodies of water. Since the river was banked on either side by rocky prominences, it was Brenston's job to steer them through. At the tops of the masts, Sis and Sass had the advantage of height and acted as lookouts, warning their captain, first mate, and crew of any troubled waters. As instructed by Norton, the beavers were to 'go with the flow,' using the dip and row rhythm established by Beatoven. So it was that, along with whatever wind Sis and Sass could catch with their sails, the Skunk Salvation Seekers slowly journeyed toward an unknown destination.

* * *

A week after they set sail, on a particularly black and cloudless evening, Celeste approached Norton, who was standing alone in the middle of the raft contemplating the night sky. She approached quietly so as not to disturb him, but he detected her distinctive musky fragrance and at once sensed her presence.

"Hello," she said simply, then continued, "Tell me what you see."

Norton, caught off-guard, was captivated. He could not look directly at her and continued his upward gaze, trying to remain composed.

"Right now I see a sliver of a moon and next to it one bright diamond of a star which —"

"Oh my, what a surprise finding both of you here, and at the same time." Mordecai strolled over to the pair. "Am I interrupting anything?"

"Why...uh...no, not really. Please join us."

Celeste, with a sweet but subtle sarcasm in her voice, said, "Norton, how thoughtful of you to invite Mordecai to join us. That way we won't be alone."

Disappointed, Norton said nothing, leaving it up to Mordecai to answer.

"True, Celeste, and isn't it splendid sharing this beautiful night with friends?"

"Why of course, Mordecai. It's just 'splendid,' as you say."

Celeste, who had been standing a little closer to Norton than was the custom among unmated skunks, had to make room for Mordecai who nudged his way between the two.

Hey, Mordy, I was just commenting to Celeste about the stars."

"Oh, yes they are beautiful and together with the moon, most interesting. Have you noticed the subtle changes they make each night?"

"Yeah. I've been curious about it. The moon and stars seem to shift their positions, ever so slightly."

"Yes, and about every thirty markings the moon grows and then shrinks and then starts growing again."

"Do you have any idea why?"

"Well, Norty, I have this theory. Perhaps the moon is a large piece of cheese being eaten by a hidden rat and the stars a path to the cheese." He raised a paw to the sky and made a sweep of his arm. "Just look at that white way."

While the cousins were engrossed in their discussion, Celeste, feeling left out, began to slowly walk away allowing her tail to gently brush against Norton. Immediately he was distracted.

"Wait Celeste, where are you going?"

"Oh, I need to get back to my kitchen duties, I'll see you again. Maybe next moon."

"Uh...okay, see you then. Bye."

"Norty, I better get going, too. Need to get back to my work space and make another star chart. See you later."

Left alone, Norton thought about what might have been and began imagining a different scenario for the next night.

"Next moon...next moon. Can I wait that long? I'll invite Celeste to join me sky-gazing. What if she says no? I think she'll say yes...otherwise why did she brush up against me with her tail? What if I'm wrong and it was only an accident? Then maybe she won't accept. Her scent drives me crazy. And the feel of her tail...so full, so soft...so silky. Wow, it made me shiver all over. I hope Mordy didn't notice. I don't need any of his advice when it comes to females. After all, he is a weasel. If we do sky-gaze next moon, I'll tell Celeste that her eyes sparkle like the stars. They're so bright, just twinkling in the moonlight. Oh, the way she met my gaze when I first saw her..."

After Mordecai left Norton standing alone in the moonlight, oblivious to the attraction developing between his cousin and Celeste, he hastened back to his work space where his draft table awaited. Once there, Mordecai began another star chart of the night sky. He had produced one per night ever since the beginning of the voyage and kept them in chronological order, numbered with small parallel lines in the upper right hand corner. The first had but a single line. With each night came another drawing and hence another line to keep track of the voyage. In this way Mordecai recorded time, despite his inability to track distance.

* * *

Heavy clouds blocked any view of the night sky for the next two moons making gazing impossible. Finally, after the night sky cleared, Norton invited Celeste to join him on deck.

"What a lovely invitation, Norton. I would be delighted. When we met the last time, there was something I wanted to show you about the sky."

"What was that?"

"Well, did you ever notice that the stars make interesting designs?"

"No, not really. Mordecai and I have been so interested in changes the stars and moon make from one sundown to the next that I never noticed."

"Maybe I can show you what I mean the next—"

"Hi Norty, where'd you disappear to after we ate?" Mordecai pushed forward between the two. "I've been looking for you."

"Been around, Mordy, guess you just didn't see me."

"Oh hi, Celeste. My compliments to you and the kitchen skunks. This dusk's meal was especially delicious. I don't know how you do it, but keep it up."

"Thanks, Mordy."

"You're more than welcome, Celeste. Well, are you all set to hear my latest moon theory, Norty?"

"Uh...sure. Go ahead. I'm listening."

But Norton was not listening, at least not at first. He was distracted by another of Celeste's exits. This time, she tickled his whiskers with the tip of her tail as she turned away from him, heading in a different direction. And her musky scent was even stronger and more captivating than ever.

"Bye...enjoy yourselves."

"Oh...bye, Celeste. See you soon...I hope."

Celeste was already out of sight by the time Norton whispered the last two words.

"Anything wrong, Norty? You look...well, I would say...forlorn."

"No, no. I'm fine. Just a little tired."

"Maybe you're working too hard. Listen, maybe my moon theory will perk you up."

"Go ahead. I'm looking forward to hearing it."

However, Norton was not looking forward to hearing another of his cousin's moon theories. His mind was elsewhere.

"Consider this, Norty...Maybe the stars are a sprinkle of diamonds scattered by the wind. And the moon might be the head of a bodiless man counting his wealth. Norty, are you even listening? You have a faraway look."

But Norton only heard part of it. "Norty, what's wrong with you, did you hear my theory or not?"

"Oh. Yeah. It was about diamonds."

"Oh, for the sake of the sun and the moon and the stars. That was only part of it. Didn't you hear me say anything about the moon being a wealthy man?"

"I guess not."

"Norty, I've never seen you so distracted. Maybe you're sick. I think you should go back to your lab space and get some rest. And I'll go back to my work space and make another blueprint, even though the sky seems flat tonight. Still need to keep count, you know, but I wonder where the stars and moon went? Sometimes they just seem to disappear."

Turning toward Norton, Mordecai said his farewell and wandering off, mulled over his theories.

Again Norton was left alone with thoughts of Celeste. "I know what I'll do. Mordy gave me a good idea. When Celeste and I finally go sky-gazing, I'll tell her that if the stars were diamonds, and I could reach the sky, I would pluck out the largest and brightest of them and give it to her. Then I'll look into her eyes and tell her they sparkle just like the stars above. And then she'll snuggle up really close...so close that our whiskers would be electrified and stand straight out. Then..."

* * *

Finally, on the thirtieth marking of the moon's growth, as recorded by Mordecai, the night sky was perfect. The full Hunter Moon was large and rosy at first, but later became a brilliant white orb suspended high in the night sky. Its beam caused the water to shimmer and cast a glow on the raft. Norton approached Celeste after the sundown meal.

"Hi, Celeste, good meal tonight."

"Thanks, I tried out a new recipe."

"It tasted wonderful."

"Glad you enjoyed it."

"I did."

"You did?"

"Uh...yes. Hey, Celeste. It's beautiful tonight, just perfect for sky-gazing. I'm on my way to the deck. Wanna come along?"

"Sure."

This time Norton guided Celeste to a different part of the raft, the one that was farthest from Mordecai's work space. Norton, who had rehearsed his diamond proposal repeatedly, thought he was ready.

"Celeste, don't you think the stars look like diamonds?"

"I never thought of them that way. I know you and Mordecai have your theories, but take a look at the stars again. I'm looking at them in a completely different way."

"You are?"

"Yes. Let me tell you what I see."

"Okay, go ahead."

"Well, I see the stars as sparkly dots. If you connect them, they make pictures. See over there?"

Celeste pointed from one star to another with one of her sharp but delicate claws. Norton was mesmerized.

"If you connect these dots, it almost looks like Mephuselah. And right there, if you connect those dots, it looks like a—"

"Hey, you two, what are you doing way over there? Mordecai bounded up and bumped Norton away from Celeste. "Did you think you would get away with sky-gazing without me on this spectacular evening?"

"Look, Mordecai. I don't mean to be rude, but that's exactly what I was trying to do."

"What?"

"Avoid you."

"Avoid me?"

Never had Norton spoken to his cousin in anything other than a jovial manner, and Mordecai was shocked.

"Norty, we're best friends, and now Celeste has joined our friendship."

"That's the problem, Mordy. Maybe I don't want that kind of friendship with Celeste."

Celeste stepped away allowing Norton and Mordecai to converse between themselves. However, this time she didn't leave. She overheard Mordecai say, "Well, then what kind of friendship *do* you want with Celeste?"

"Don't be silly. You're a weasel. You know precisely what I mean."

"Oh! So my uninterested cousin—the one who professed not to care about skunks of the opposite sex, the one who said he would never mate—is finally interested."

"Yes, now that you understand, would you please leave us alone?"

"Okay, okay, I'm leaving...heh, heh. Just let me know how it all turns out."

"Sure, Mordy. You'll be the first to know."

With that, Mordecai left and Celeste came closer to Norton, making sure their fur was touching. Each felt the warmth of the other and snuggled in.

"Celeste, what were you explaining to me before...well, before Mordy arrived?"

"Ummm...oh yes, that feels good."

"What feels good?"

"You know, being so close."

"Listen, Celeste. I don't know what you wanted to tell me about the stars, but tonight I wanted to tell you...well, if I could, I would give you all the stars in the sky. They twinkle just like your eyes and they look like diamonds. I guess what I'm saying is I would give you all the diamonds in the sky if I could."

The diamond proposal didn't come out exactly as Norton had rehearsed, but Celeste understood nonetheless. She flushed in response to Norton's words, the heat of the moment and the romance of the evening.

"Oh Captain, my Captain, I am so flattered."

"Celeste, I want you to be my forever-mate."

"I've been waiting for you to ask but your cousin..."

"Yeah, I know. That's why I finally had to tell him to leave us alone."

"I'm so glad you did, and now that I've accepted your proposal—"

"You have?"

"Of course, silly. It'll be obvious soon enough, so we better tell your cousin or his feelings will be hurt. You did tell him he'd be the first to know. I heard you."

Before making their commitment announcement to Mordecai, Norton gave Celeste his most prized possession, the acorn necklace containing the formula to his secret compound. He slipped it from around his neck to hers, entrusting her with the skunk solution and with it the future of Skunkdom.

The two then hastened to find Mordecai who was busy in his work space.

"Oh my. Last I saw you two, you wanted to be alone. Please come in."

"Mordy, Celeste, and I want you to be the first to know that we've made a commitment to one another to be forever-mates."

"Wonderful news. Congratulations. You were meant for each other, after all. It was in the stars, wasn't it?" He chuckled.

Celeste said, "Mordecai, the moon is still out. Let's all go sky-gazing again. Your focus has been the moon, but my focus has been the stars. I was just beginning to show Norton what I discovered when you, well, interrupted... So now I would like to show both of you."

"Okay, Celeste. Let's go."

As they made their way to an open part of the raft, Celeste said, "I was starting to show Norton how the stars make patterns. See, if you connect that star to that one, and that one to that one, it kind of looks like an outline of Mephuselah. If you connect those six stars, it looks a little like the outline of a tree."

"You're right, Celeste," said Mordy. "I was so busy focusing on my moon theories that I never considered what you just showed us about the stars. Fact is, my latest moon theory has to do with its relationship to the sun, which I've stayed up after dawn to study. Yours is indeed a different approach and an important one, because it'll help us to remember our homes back in the East and Westphalia."

"Hey, Mordy, how about you make blueprints of the star connections. That way we can share them with the passengers and crew."

"Great idea, Norty."

So every night after the last meal was served, Mordecai shared his blueprints for diversion, just as one would a family album.

"Look at this blueprint. Don't you see that tyrant Bubo?"

"Yes, it looks exactly like him, that miserable bird. He's the one that drove us out of our homes."

"Yes, that's true Norty, but if he hadn't, we wouldn't be having this adventure."

"Celeste, How about this one? It looks like the old Hubbard House in the middle of the forest, the one where Norty passed his infamous farts."

On and on it went in a never ending stream of recollection.

~7~

Problems

It was the eve of a full Beaver Moon when Beatoven swaggered up to Norton, demanding a moment of his time.

"What is it Beats?"

"Well, Captain Norton, I need to tell ya that the rowing rhythm is only good for jus' so long. After that, our forward progress gets slower and slower. I tried changing the rhythm but nothing helps."

"What about using the Sis and Sass sails?"

"We were, up 'til now, but using the sails don't get us as far as rowing does. And the other night me and Brenston...we talked. Said there ain't been much wind for the last five of them blueprints. Fact is, even though Sis's sail is up all the time, Sass lowered hers 'cuz it kept flapping around so much she couldn't stay on top of it."

"Well, that is a problem, Beats. Let me speak with First Mate Mordecai, and I'll see what he thinks."

That evening Norton had a long conversation with Mordecai.

After hearing of their dilemma, Mordecai said, "Hmmm, this is indeed a quandary. There are ten rowing beavers on each side. Right?"

"Yup, twenty in all," Norton confirmed.

"They dip and row at the same time to a rhythm selected by Beats. Right?"

"Right again, but they are fatigued despite Beats trying out different rowing rhythms."

"Norty, as I see it, the beavers aren't getting any breaks no matter what rhythm they use. No wonder they're all tuckered out. The challenge at hand is not changing the rowing rhythm, but rather changing the motion method itself, so the crew can have some down time."

"You're absolutely right, Mordy. Let's give them some leeway. But how?"

"I don't know. I need time to think about it."

"Okay. I'll tell Beats you're working on the problem. How long do you figure it'll take before you come up with one of your inventive ideas?"

"Probably most of the night. Let's meet again before daybreak."

Norton went back to Beatoven and the crew to give them words of encouragement. Mordecai went to his makeshift drafting table in the far left corner of the raft's bow. He pondered for some time, but nothing came to mind.

"Ummm, well, there's only one last thing to do. It's time for another Aunt Agram. What was the last thing Norton said? He said, 'give them some leeway.'"

Mordecai began the word unscramble, starting with the first word. He wrote G-I-V-E and V-I-E-G, then E-V-I-G, then I-E-V-G.

"No, nothing at all."

Next he tried the word *them* and wrote H-E-M-T, then M-E-H-T then T-H-M-E. Still nothing came to mind. Lastly he tried *leeway*. He wrote down Y-E-E-L-W-A, then E-E-L-Y-A-W, and finally tried spelling it backwards: Y-A-W-E-E-L.

"Nothing there either." Mordecai was discouraged until he thought again about the spelling Y-A-W-E-E-L.

"Wait a minute, there might be something I can do with Y-A-W-E-E-L. Perhaps if I translate the *ya* into *yes* and *weel* to *wheel*? That's it! Yes, wheel."

Suddenly Mordecai conceived of a new motion method. Mumbling to himself in hushed tones, Mordecai described what he envisioned. "When there's no wind, Sass shall be the center of a large wheel with her eight legs extended outward. Eight of the twenty beavers will grasp one leg each with their left paw forward. Putting their right paw around the beaver next to them, they form a circle. Next, the circle is put in an upright position. Now...where to put the wheel. Hmmm...I think it should be in the stern. If it's in the bow, the view will be blocked."

The more Mordecai mused, the more outlandish his notion became.

"Twine made from some of Sass's strong-as-steel spider silk can be braided together and used to attach the wheel to the raft. More twine can be used to help the beavers hold on to Sass's legs. The beavers will face inward with their hind ends outward. They'll take turns, no longer dipping and rowing continuously, but rather taking turns paddling. As the wheel rotates, each beaver's tail will dip into the water and paddle one at a time, but only once before the next revolution. The raft will then be propelled in a forward movement. The remaining twelve beavers can rest until their shift. So if I am counting right, there would be two shifts of eight. That makes sixteen, with four beavers left over as alternates."

Now, having thought it all out, Mordecai yelled, "Eureka! I'll call it a paddle wheel. Our raft will be the NBC Paddle Wheel instead of the NBC Barge. Norty? Norty! Come quickly. I've had a breakthrough."

Excitedly Mordecai explained the new motion method to Norton who was, as always, amazed at his cousin's brilliance.

"You've done it again, Mordy. I knew I could count on you."

"Speaking of count, we need a way to mark when the wheel has made a complete turn. I need to know how many turns it takes before the first shift tires and it's time for the second shift to take over. Hmmm, really this should be easy. All I need to do is make a mark with blueberry ink on one of the twines extending from Sass's legs. Each time I see the marked twine, I will make note of it."

At first Beatoven, Brenston, the beaver crew, Sis and even Sass were excited about trying out the new motion method. Unfortunately, Mordecai's invention was a success only in his dreams. When they tried it out, Sass became so dizzy she fainted. And the pain in her legs caused by the stretching was unbearable.

It was an impossible scheme, and the crew grew despondent. For about fourteen blueprints, the Sis and Sass sails captured barely enough wind to propel the raft forward. When the wind stopped blowing and the beavers stopped rowing, the raft began to drift aimlessly... into winter.

"Captain Norton, there's still no wind. If we go back to dip and row, the crew will jus' tire out again."

"You're right, Beats. But we can't continue this drifting. The beavers need to start rowing, at least until Mordecai comes up with another method or the wind picks up."

Norton sought out Mordecai to further discuss the situation.

Mordecai shook his head in defeat. "Norty, I keep trying to invent a different motion method but so far, no new ideas. I think we need to discuss the problem with all the passengers."

So the captain and first mate gathered the passengers mid-deck.

Norton explained the difficulties of the crew. He was about to ask all on board to help First Mate Mordecai come up with a plan, but he was cut short by Mordecai. "I see dark clouds ahead. Soon enough there'll be wind but it won't be friendly. We need to prepare. It's gotten colder. My fur is thicker and you can see that I'm almost all white now. I suspect that if you check, you'll see that your fur is also thicker. Winter is upon us."

The beavers and skunks began licking their coats to determine if any changes had occurred.

"Say, Mordecai, my fur sure is thicker and it tastes kinda salty."

Norton said, "Beats, that's very interesting. I suspect we've entered different waters that are larger and deeper than we've experienced, waters that are saline. So listen up, there's bad news and good news. The bad news is that we must not drink even a drop of this water, no matter how thirsty we are. The good news is we've traveled far enough to reach an important larger body of water. We must proceed with caution and conserve the fresh river water we brought with us."

There was a worrisome buzz.

Norton hushed the crew. "Beavers, skunks, Sis and Sass: the need to find a new motion method has been, until now, our main concern. But, unfortunately, we have another. Our food stock has diminished more than expected. The pantry is well guarded by Celeste and some of the kitchen crew skunks. They've been very careful about food distribution at each meal. You may have noted that seconds are no longer being served. Celeste, please tell the crew what you found."

Unaccustomed to speaking in front of large gatherings, Celeste's voice was hesitant. "Um, well... while I was counting the food supplies, I noticed that some of the dried corn and berries were spilled and scattered. Also there were animal droppings, smaller than a skunk's or a weasel's."

When she finished speaking, Celeste wrapped herself up in her own tail and drew closer to Norton.

"Since I trust all of you," Norton said, "there must be some other animal nibbling from the larder. Apparently we have a stowaway. Considering the size of the droppings, it's a very small animal and can hide easily. So this, my fellow passengers, is Problem Number Two. We need to find the stowaway at once. I'll help Mordecai work on ideas for another motion method. Do I have any volunteers who will search from bow to mid-deck?"

Celeste immediately said, "I will Captain Norton."

"Okay, Celeste. How about if Sis and Sass accompany you?"

"We'll do it," the sisters said in unison.

"Brenston and Beatoven, the two of you can search from stern to mid-deck. The rest of the beavers can take a break. You all know your duties, so be off and report back here before sunrise."

"Just a minute Captain Norton." Beatoven said. "How's about you and Mordecai replace me and Brenston in this here search? The two of us need to meet with the beavers and discuss some other important matters."

"What matters, Beats?"

"Well, us beavers think it's time we let yous know what our needs are, instead of you guessing and getting it all wrong."

"Gee, Beats, I thought we were doing a good job for you beavers."

"Well, we want to have a say-so in things, being that we're doing all the work."

"Sure, sure, I guess. Go ahead. Mordecai and I will take your place during the search, won't we Mordecai?"

"You're the captain. It's your decision. So yes, let the beavers have their meeting. And as you said, we'll all meet up before sunrise."

Beatoven gathered the beaver crew. "We all knew this would be hard work, but now we're finding out that it's really, *really* hard. Sometimes it's downright exhausting. I see how tired you guys get. We gotta talk to Captain Norton and Mordecai again, 'cuz we still don't have any other way to go forward except by rowing with our tails. There's gotta be a better way. Plus, we never get any breaks—even when we're sick."

In unison, the crew beat their flat tails on the raft's deck, indicating their approval of Beatoven's remarks.

"Just hold on," said Brenston. "Come on, Captain Norton and Mordecai tried a different method for us, but it just don't work."

Some of the beavers buzzed their agreement.

"Yeah, Brenston, but don't go thinking they did it to help us. They did it so they could get where they want faster, not 'cuz of *our* needs. Also Captain Norton and First Mate Mordecai were probably thinking that we would just quit if they didn't do something. Then where would they be? I'll tell you! Up a crick without a paddle."

Brenston spoke out again, defending his captain and first mate. "Yous is thinking about this the wrong way. I heard Captain Norton tell Mordecai about the beavers being so tired and how we need a new motion method."

"All right," said Beatoven. "Ya win on that point, but even though we agreed to join up and help, I think Captain Norton and Mordecai should show us some thanks."

The beavers again beat their tails. Brenston, the sole beaver defending Norton and Mordecai broke in.

"Beavers, don't go forgetting why we're here. The skunks were kicked out of the forest by that miserable Bubo Owl. The skunks have been our friends for as long as I can think back on it. Why, there's a story my Gran' Dad told me 'bout when a bunch of beavers got sick from sawing down some poison oak trees. It was the skunk neighbors that took care of the beavers. And now it's our turn to help them. We're giving them a chance to escape. You agreed to help them build this here raft. Plus, yous wanted adventure, so you signed up to be the crew. Weren't we all bored with dam building back home? This was our ticket to adventure. Besides, it was only a matter of time before Bubo came down hard on us."

Swayed by Brenston's reasoning, the beavers buzzed a supportive response.

"You're right, Brenston," Beats said. "But we di'n't know how long or hard the trip would be. And we still don't. We're bigger than the skunks. We need more food. It's *us* doing the heavy labor. I wanna know what Captain Norton and Mordecai do all night while we work so hard without a single break."

"You listen here, Beatoven. Mordecai is our only inventor. And he won't never give up. I betcha he'll come up with some kinda new motion method soon enough. If you wanna know what Captain Norton is up to, I'll tell you. He's doing some kinda experiment with that solution stuff he found. I seen him drinking different amounts of it every night. It makes his stomach puff up and then he has to fart real bad. I think the captain's trying to teach hisself how much of the stuff to drink and seeing if he can control how fast it comes outta him. Also, don't forget, he brought along all his potions and lotions, and even used some when one of yous got sick or hurt."

The beavers were now banging their tails in unison. Beatoven was embarrassed but finally gained his composure. "Beavers, I'm not trying to be ornery. Let's see what we can do to make it better for us guys. Like a little more food, some rest breaks, and knowing that if we get sick, we get time off 'til we get better. Let's organize and choose whose going to tell Captain Norton what we need."

"Yeah, Beats. Now that makes sense. First let's see a show of paws for all who want to be represented by you and me."

All the beavers slapped their tails and raised their right paws.

"Then we're all agreed. Next, we need to name our group," said Brenston.

The beavers were thinking, but it was Beatoven who made the first suggestion. "I know! Beavers Against Disadvantages? We can shorten it to B.A.D."

Quickly, before the beavers could respond, Brenston said, "No, too negative. We need to be positive. We're a brotherhood, not just a complaint department."

The beavers buzzed.

"How 'bout, we call it the Amalgamated Brotherhood of Benevolent Beavers?"

Beatoven, feeling that his position of authority had been usurped by Brenston, nonetheless acknowledged his agreement. "Yeah, I guess that name will do. From now on we are the Amalgamated Brotherhood of Benevolent Beavers."

From the back of the group one of the beavers chimed in, "Yeah, now that's what I'm talking about."

This was applauded by a loud slapping of tails.

~ 8 ~

Celeste Makes a Discovery

Celeste, Sis, and Sass, started searching in the larder located in the raft's bow. While Celeste looked in the food storage bins, Sis and Sass scrambled along the kitchen's perimeter.

"Whatever it is, it must have been here because—"

"There are telltale crumbs in the crevices."

"Sass, do you always need to finish my sentence?"

"Yeah, cause you never give me a chance. You think 'cuz you came first, you get to go first."

Celeste interrupted a bit impatiently. "Ladies, stop your bickering. We need to concentrate on the task. If the food thief dropped crumbs along the perimeter, it may have created a trail. So let's follow the crumbs."

Sis and Sass tailed Celeste, who led the hunt. They found a trail, and it ended almost at mid-deck, not far from the Sis and Sass sails. Celeste saw movement within the threads of Sis's sail. Upon closer examination, she realized it was the tail of an animal hiding behind the mast, attempting to blend in. The animal stilled as Celeste crept closer.

When she was within reach, Celeste opened her mouth and grabbed the tail between her teeth. The animal wiggled but was unable to escape Celeste's strong hold. Whip-like, Celeste snapped the long tail and swirled the animal around.

"Ouch! Stop."

Suddenly, Celeste was nose-to-nose with a small mouse whose tail was still gripped in her mouth. Sis and Sass scuttled over in time to hear the mouse say, "Let me go. Please. I promise not to run away."

"I'll make sure you don't," said Sass, giving the small mouse a spider bite strong enough to temporarily sedate it. "Celeste, what do you want to do with it?"

"Well, it will soon be sunrise, and that's when Captain Norton said we should reconvene. Let's find him before the meeting begins. I'm sure he'll know what to do. By then the mouse might be awake and able to give us an explanation."

Carefully transporting the mouse in her mouth, Celeste and the two spiders left to find Norton, who was engrossed in a discussion with Mordecai. Celeste approached and gently tugged his extended stripeless tail.

Startled, Norton turned. "What?"

No explanation was needed once he saw Celeste carrying the small dead-looking mouse. "Looks like you found our intruder and solved Problem Number Two. How did it die?"

"It's not dead, just stunned. Sass gave it a little bite so it wouldn't run away."

"Wow, Sass! I knew your venom would come in handy one day. Thank you both for helping Celeste.

"Oh, it was nothing, Captain Norton," the sisters said together.

"Well, what should we do with it? What do you think, Mordecai?"

Mordecai was sizing up the mouse and thinking it would make a delicious snack. "Well, we're all supposed to meet up again before sunrise. Let's present the mouse to all on board before any decisions are made."

"Excellent. And it will be a good time to publicly thank Celeste, Sis, and Sass for their heroic efforts."

* * *

The animals crowded at mid-deck as the sun peeked above the horizon. Captain Norton, Mordecai, Celeste, Sis, and Sass stood in front, facing the beaver crew and the skunk passengers. A small, gray mouse lay in front of Celeste on a lacy piece of web fabricated by Sis. Several of the crew eyed the mouse hungrily, almost as if it might be a special offering. As the effects of Sass's venom wore off, the mouse regained consciousness. It rubbed its eyes, wrinkled its nose, and twitched its whiskers.

"So, you've found me out. Now what?" the mouse asked brazenly.

"Hush, mouse. As captain of this vessel, I'll be asking the questions. But before we deal with you, I need to explain to all on board exactly how you were found."

Norton explained how Celeste apprehended the mouse and how Sis and Sass helped.

"First, how shall we honor Celeste, Sis, and Sass for their wit and creativity in locating this intruder?" Norton asked the gathered animals. "And second, what shall we do with the mouse? Any suggestions?"

Beatoven took the lead. "Captain Norton, the beavers have taken a vote. Brenston and I will be the voice of all the beavers from now on. We'll speak as one voice, that of the Amalgamated Brotherhood of Benevolent Beavers."

Captain Norton and Mordecai glanced at each other, astonished by the announcement, which seemed abrupt and out of place.

"Well, this is a surprise," Norton responded. "We can discuss the merits of your brotherhood after we honor the ladies and decide what course of action to take regarding our little stowaway. Again, I have asked ask *all* of you for your suggestions."

Norton gave the passengers and crew a chance to respond, but no responses were forthcoming. All were silent.

"Since there are no suggestions at this time, please give it some thought. We'll meet again at moonrise. In the meantime let's eat and get a good day's rest."

Some of the beavers, being very hungry, yelled, "Yeah! Let's eat."

Sis and Sass scurried away to dine on the few insects stuck in the web of their respective sails. Celeste returned to the larder to ready the evening meal. Brenston, Beatoven, and the beaver crew dispersed, albeit begrudgingly, knowing they were obligated to propel the raft. Only Norton, Mordecai, and the stowaway remained at mid-deck.

Before him, sitting upon the cloth made by Sis and Sass, was what Mordecai envisioned as a treat. He salivated and licked his chops. "Mmmm, all I need is a little sauce."

The mouse shook with fear.

"Mordy, don't even think of that as a solution, despite there being a decline in the pantry."

"Yeah, I know, but it's tempting. And besides, I would share it with you."

"Not interested. We need to hear how and why this little critter came aboard. So what's your story, Mousey?"

"My name isn't Mousey. It's Mousella."

"All right then, Mousella. Tell us how you got on board."

"Well, it's your own fault, *Captain* Norton. That's what the crew calls you, right?"

"Right. Now explain."

"I knew you even before you became Captain Norton Bulymur of the Skunk Salvation Seekers. I knew you when you were just plain Norton, the chemist who polluted the forest. I knew you when the Hubbard House was despoiled with one of your hideous farts. I was there. I was one of the mice blinded by your irresponsibility. I didn't know what to do, so I used my keen sense of smell to follow you."

Norton was incredulous. "Oh, my stars! You followed me? I had no idea. I've felt guilty ever since the incident. Fact is, I experienced a period of the same blindness after the explosion in my lab. It was frightening enough for me. I can't begin to imagine what you went through, being so small."

"Well, it actually wasn't too bad. My eyesight never was that good anyway."

"That doesn't matter. To be blinded, even for a little while...you're a brave little mouse and, I must say, resourceful as well. Mordy, we can't abandon the little thing."

"The name's Mousella."

"Sorry, I forgot. Mousella."

"But, Norty, even you said our larder has been reduced. We need to conserve our food."

"I know, but it...I mean Mousella...can't eat *that* much."

"Well, it has. You heard what Celeste told us."

"Listen, Mordy, we can all eat a little less, just until we find a new food source."

"New food source?"

"Yes. We found our stowaway and solved Problem Number Two, but we still have a food shortage. That, Mordy, is Problem Number Three. There must be other things we can eat besides what we brought on board. Get creative, Mordy. See what you can figure out."

"Okay, Norty, I'll try, but—"

"You mean I can stay?" the little mouse squeaked.

"Yes...er, welcome aboard, Mousella."

"You won't be sorry. I promise to find a way to earn my keep. No more stealing from the larder. I'll happily eat any leftover crumbs."

Mordecai's stomach rumbled loudly. "There aren't any leftover crumbs," he grumbled.

"Mordy, don't be negative," Norton scolded.

"Maybe I can help Celeste with meal cleanup," Mousella squeaked. "And don't forget, I'm the smallest animal on board. My whiskers are extra sensitive, so I'm really good at perceiving details around me. You never know when I might be needed."

Despite Norton asking everyone to consider how to honor the ladies and what to do about the mouse, the passengers and crew gave it no thought. The passengers remained uninvolved in all decisions relating to the voyage, relying on the decisions of their captain. As for the beaver crew, they left all decision-making up to Brenston and Beatoven. Driven by selfish motivation, the two focused solely on the needs of the beavers and had a meeting of their own before the one scheduled by Norton. The purpose of their meeting was to draft a proposal regarding beaver working conditions. When they were done, together, they delivered the proposal to Norton.

Norton and Mordecai were discussing the current situations when they heard a knock at the door.

"Please…Brenston, Beatoven, come in," Norton said in a friendly tone. "What can we do for you?"

"Captain Norton…me and Beats have a list of our needs we'd like to talk about. Number one, us guys are bigger than the skunks, so we need more food. Number two, this rowing business is tough work. Like I said before, we need some other way to make this here raft go forward. Number three, when we get sick we need to be taken care of. And number four, we don't get no rest. We need some time off."

"Look, we'll honor your requests as best we can. Mordecai has been working on an alternate motion method, but it may take some time. As for medical attention, haven't I provided that special ointment for tail aches?"

"Yeah, but now it's not just about tail aches."

"What do you mean?"

"This new salty water...well, we're not used to it. Our tails are sore and the salt in the water stings. We need something that'll work better. Maybe a stronger ointment"

Frustrated, Norton rubbed his head, thinking that this was yet another quagmire, adding to the several he was already trying to handle.

"Okay, I'm certain we can come up with something. But your request for more food presents a different challenge. Our pantry supplies are shrinking daily. We need to find another food source. And we have another mouth to feed now, small though it is."

"What do ya mean, another mouth to feed?"

Still fraught with guilt over the temporary blinding of Mousella, Norton recounted the little mouse's story and his decision to allow her to remain on board.

Beatoven who tried to be attentive during the conversation between Norton and Brenston finally became agitated enough to interrupt. "Listen, does Mordecai even have time to work on a new rowing method now that he also needs to get us more food?"

"Why of course, Beats. It's just a matter of time before he comes up with something. He's very smart."

Beatoven continued, "What about our tails?"

"That's up to me. I'll experiment with my oint-
ments to find a new salve. By the way, I'm glad you
came to me to discuss your concerns. As your captain, I assure you I'll do everything I can, as fast
as I can. We realize how important the beavers are,
and we pledge to work with you."

So with that, the beavers thanked Norton and
left. They had intended to report directly to the
crew, but first they had a heated discussion between themselves.

"Hey what's with that Captain Norton anyway?"
Beatoven began. "He asks us what we should do
about the mouse, and then he does his own thing.
What's up with that?"

"Beats, cool it. We might not agree with all he
does but, like, he is our captain. You know what
I mean?"

"Let me tell you something, Brenston. I still
don't like it, and I don't think the rest of the crew
will either."

"Look Beats, forget about the mouse. We need
to look out for us beavers. I'm not worried about no
mouse, I'm worried about us... get me? We gotta cut
a deal with Captain Norton, and that's what counts."

"Humph. Okay, but I won't wait too long. In the
meantime that mouse — what's her name —"

"Mousella."

"Yeah, Mousella. She better find a way to earn
her keep."

"I'm sure she will. Look, I'm hungry. How about
you? Let's go eat and try to get our fill before the
next meeting."

When the meal was over, all met mid-deck to congratulate and thank Celeste, Sis, and Sass. Then came Norton's announcement regarding Mousella.

"Let me introduce Mousella, our new passenger."

A low grumbling could be heard amongst the beaver crew, but no one made any outright objections. Norton quickly redirected everyone's attention. "The winds are picking up, and the storm predicted by Mordecai is not far off. So I call an end to this meeting. Let's all get busy."

Sis and Sass scampered off to their lookout posts. Celeste and Mousella rushed away to secure the food storage bins. Mordecai hurried back to his work space to figure how to protect the beavers' tails before they got sores and needed an ointment. He also needed to think about another food source and continue his work on a new motion method. Norton went to his makeshift lab where he was refining the process of gas emissions. The beavers, though disappointed about not yet having a new motion method, returned to their rowing positions with Beatoven commanding the bow and Brenston at the stern.

~ 9 ~

The Storm

The Salvation Seekers were fast asleep during the day of the next moon, as the cold winds first noted by Mordecai escalated to gale proportions. Sis and Sass were the first to awaken to the howling winds and the sting of frigid hail. Despite their strength, the sisters' sails were powerless against the fierce winds that had stirred up the sea. Up on their masts, Sis and Sass could see high, white-capped waves and a large swell in the distance, rolling toward them.

The winds were wailing, and Sis yelled to Sass, "We better warn everyone below. Start blinking."

"What do you mean...start?" Sass hollered back, "I've been blinking. But it's raining too hard. No one below can see our warning lights."

"What should we do? Any bright ideas? You better come up with something, Sis, or we're doomed."

Just then a large gust of wind ripped through Sis's sail, making a tear. She scurried down her pole, unraveling the sail's silk thread as she went to prevent further tearing of the strands. Sis screamed for Sass to do the same.

"Hurry, before your sail's destroyed."

"Toyed?"

"No, destroyed."

"Okay. I'll meet you down below."

Back on deck, the sisters found themselves standing in a pile of their own silk thread.

"Okay, smarty. Now what?"

"I've got an idea. Start winding the thread into a ball and then hoist it on your back."

"What good will that do? You and your brilliant ideas...This better be good."

"Don't get snippy with me, Sass. Just do what I say."

"You're so bossy."

"Enough arguing! Just do it; the swell is getting closer."

After the silk was wound and on their backs, Sis showed Sass how to use the silk to tie each passenger to various protrusions in and around the raft.

Beginning with Norton, Sis wound her cord around the captain until he was fastened to a piece of wood jutting up from the floor of his makeshift lab.

Norton opened his eyes, disoriented. "Sis, let me go. Stop. What do you think you're doing?"

"Sorry, Captain Norton. There's no time to explain."

She scuttled off to bind Mordecai, who also protested. While Sis secured Norton and Mordecai, Sass did the same to Celeste and Mousella. Then they shared the task of securing the skunk passengers and beaver crew. Just as they were ready to fasten the last two of the twenty-member rowing crew, the balls of silk cord came to an abrupt end. Sis and Sass were horrified as the two unsecured beavers were snatched away by the foamy spray of the large swell they had seen in the distance. It happened so fast they didn't even hear Benjamin's and Barclay's piercing cries.. All that was left was the lingering sound of the howling wind.

Once the sound of the wailing wind died down, it was replaced by the screams of the passengers as they struggled to free themselves from the silken bonds Sis and Sass had used to secure them.

"Sis, see what a ruckus you caused?"

"Shut up, we need to give everyone a goodnight kiss before we spin some new thread to secure ourselves."

"What do you mean, goodnight kiss? Have you lost your mind?"

"No, dummy. With a bit of our venom, they'll sleep through the storm."

There was nothing more for Sass to say. She followed Sis's instruction, and the two injected each passenger with a small amount of potent poison. When they were finished, each spun enough silk to secure themselves to their masts. Transfixed, they watched the angry sea smash against the raft.

The small vessel pitched forward, backward, sideways, and vertically in a seemingly endless ride, devoid of amusement. Night turned to day and all on board slept, including Sis and Sass.

* * *

It might have been a single long day. It might have been several suns or moons. No one would know how long the storm lasted, without Mordecai's blueprints. At nightfall, Sis and Sass awoke and were overcome by grief and guilt over the loss of Benjamin and Barclay, the beavers who had been snatched by the cruel sea.

"What will we tell everyone, especially the beaver crew? They've lost two of their own," said Sis.

"I don't know. But since you're older and wiser than I, as you always like to remind me," said Sass, "I'll leave the telling up to you."

"Thanks a lot."

The sedative effect of the Sis and Sass kisses began to wear off, just as the ravaged seas were subsiding. The night sky, although visible, was cloudy. The sea was flat, and there was no wind. All was still.

Norton, the first to awaken, slowly looked around. Despite feeling groggy, he noted the raft's disarray. When he attempted to move, the silk twine pressed into his fur and cut into his skin. He struggled to free himself. "What's going on? Help! Someone untie me."

Slowly the rest of the passengers and crew began to awaken. Cries of panic, frustration, anger, and fear could be heard from different parts of the raft. The sisters got busy untying all on board and re-winding their silk into rucksacks to hoist on their backs.

When all were untied, Norton brought them all together. "My friends and fellow travelers, it is with great sorrow that we must say farewell to two members of our group who, as Sis and Sass have recounted, succumbed to the storm. Let us take a moment to remember them and pray silently that their suffering was minimal."

Sniffles and some outright crying, including Norton's weeping, could be heard. Once Norton composed himself, he again took command.

"Despite our grief, we must remain focused on our mission to find a new homeland and start a new life. The sisters saved us by binding us to the NBC Barge. The same thread that has guided and directed our voyage was used to bind us, albeit for our safety. Now that very thread will be used once again to help carry us to a new place, a new home, and a new destiny."

"Listen Sis, I'm exhausted and way too tired to begin spinning new sails now."

"Did I ask you to? Stop complaining Sass."

"There you go, correcting me, always correcting me."

"Am not."

"Are too."

"Okay, drop it already. There isn't even a decent wind in any direction to speak of, so new spinning isn't even needed right now. Besides, we still each have a full ball of silk on our backs. We can re-weave the sails from that."

"Well, that's a relief. You could have saved me the worry by mentioning that right away."

"I could never save *you* from worry. You always find something to worry about."

"Do not."

"Do too."

"Stop this nonsense. We need to resume our lookout positions. Go. Climb your mast."

"There you go bossing me again."

"Well, thanks a lot. Where would we all be if I hadn't told you what to do with your silk thread? Wasn't it my idea to use the silk from our sails to tie everyone up?"

"Yeah, Sis, but you always like spinning yourself into some kind of turmoil."

"It was the storm that spun the turmoil, not me, you royal pain in my you-know-what. There goes my warning light, and it's getting redder and hotter by the minute. You make me so angry. No wonder Mom nicknamed you Sass."

"She did that because Sassafras was too hard for you to pronounce."

Sass gave Sis a smirk and they parted if for no other reason than to get away from each other, climbing their respective masts to resume lookout duties.

The first thing Norton did was reorganize his lab. Then he resumed studying the effects of the skunk solution on gas production, paying special attention to emissions control. The chemical solution itself was kept in a waterproof storage container, same as the fresh water brought from Westphalia, all of which, fortunately, had remained unharmed by the storm.

Mordecai put his jumbled work space back in order and began the process of inventing some kind of protective gear for beaver tails. He divided his time between the protection of the beavers, thinking about how to find another food source, and developing a new motion method.

The beavers resumed their positions as crew members under the direction of Beatoven and Brenston. After discovering that little was left in the larder because the storm had blown half of it away, Celeste, Mousella and the skunks prepared what might have been one of their last meals... had it not been for a discovery.

~ 10 ~

The Isles of Ill

The raft entered boggy waters where the air was misty with a faint foul smell. And the sea, now shallow, was more difficult to navigate.

Sass double blinked to Sis. "Do you see what I see?"

"Not sure. It looks like several islands."

"Yeah, but I've never seen anything like these. One of them appears to be floating on top of the water, bobbing away, while another seems to be sinking. And I think the third has already sunk, but I can barely see it since the water is so cloudy."

"We better turn on our bright beams and warn the captain."

Sis and Sass began blinking three dots followed by three dashes and then again three dots.

Celeste was looking up at the night sky, hoping to find her favorite group of stars, when she noticed the emergency signals coming from Sis and Sass. She ran first to Norton, who ran to Mordecai, who ran to the other skunk families, who finally ran to Brenston and Beatoven, who then told the rest of the beaver crew. They all rushed to mid-deck and were joined by the sisters, who came down from their perches to report their discovery.

"Sisters, what is it? What's wrong? Why the distress signals?"

"Well, Captain Norton, Sass and I saw strange looking islands," said Sis.

Then the sisters took turns describing what they saw,

"There are three islands, all about the same size and shape."

"They look a little like walnut halves."

"Sis, you forgot to tell them about some kind of divide running down the middle."

"Thanks Sass. I was just about to say that when you interrupted me. Also there's more. Only one of the islands is really an island."

"Yeah, the other one is sinking."

"And you forgot to say that one has already sunk."

"You always have to have the last word, don't you, Sis?"

"Girls, stop quarreling," Norton commanded. "This is indeed important news."

Then Brenston spoke up."Also, Captain, something else. It's getting even harder to row. There's stringy stuff in the water and it keeps getting tangled in our tails."

"Brenston, why didn't you bring this to my attention sooner?"

"'Cuz you were so busy, I didn't want to say nothin'."

"Tell me more about the substance."

"It's kinda brown, and thick, and I seen it growing straight up under the water. I think it's coming from the bottom of the sea."

Norton became very excited, momentarily forgetting about the warning signals. "Did you save any? This might be another food source for us."

"Nope. But there's so much, I can easily get some more."

Norton was thrilled at this prospect. "Well, that's good news. Mordy, what do you think? Should we taste some and see if it's safe?"

"We have no choice, but I should be the one to try it. If it's poisonous, no use both of us getting sick."

"Good point, Mordy."

"And if it is poisonous and I do get sick, I hope you have a potion that makes me better."

"Well, I think I have something that might work. Back in Westphalia I discovered a plant that made my stomach heave after I chewed its roots. It caused me to vomit everything I had eaten earlier that night. So if anything doesn't feel right after you've eaten some of the plants, you can take a chew of the root."

"Thanks, Norty. Sounds delightful."

Brenston communicated Norton's plan to the beaver crew. "Listen up, beavers. Captain Norton needs some of that plant stuff what keeps getting stuck on our tails. Thinks it might be a new kinda food. So dip your tails in, and let's get us some."

Beatoven gave the count. "Ready. Set. Tails down. Ready. Set. Tails up. Okay, take a look-see at your tails. Anyone pull up them plants?"

"Yeah, our tails are full of the junk."

"Okay, that's the first part. Now ya gotta scrape it off with those claws of yours. Then Captain Norton and Mordecai can take it from there. Let's be hopeful."

"Ahem," Sis interjected. "Captain, we better decide about the islands Sass and I discovered."

Norton turned his attention back to the throng of skunks and beavers awaiting his decision.

"We need to determine the nature of this new land mass. Who knows? Perhaps the floating island is destined to be our new home. But first we must explore its vegetation and inhabitants. The air has a strange smell, which might be coming from the underwater plants or something else. So the island needs to be investigated."

Since the beavers kept getting their tails stuck on the water weeds, and the skunks were not the strongest of swimmers, it was Mousella, the smallest of the animals, who volunteered to scout the eerie island.

"Don't worry Captain Norton, I have a cousin, twice removed, who was a river rat, and I've inherited his swimming genes. I'll keep my nose close to the ground, scan the island, and report back before daybreak.

* * *

It didn't take long for Mousella to navigate the dense growth of plants—some brown, others green—stemming from the bottom of the murky sea. However, when she reached the strange floating island, it was a struggle to get a paw-hold, since the isle was gently bouncing.

Mousella grabbed the stringy plant life growing between the land mass and the water. Then she hoisted herself onto the isle, timidly crept ashore, and shook the chilly water off her back. She looked first to the left and then to the right, noting the gentle curve of the island's perimeter. The ground underfoot felt soft with a spongy texture, and the misty air was damp. Bravely, Mousella moved forward, using her whiskers to feel the way.

After her eyes adjusted to the damp haze, Mousella saw what appeared to be many trees, all with long stringy branches, growing flat and horizontally along the gray and undulating ground rather than vertically.

"Hmmm, very strange. I wonder why the trees are growing in this unnatural manner. Maybe once they were upright but then something flattened them. Or maybe they grow in this peculiar manner because this is a peculiar island."

She had never seen anything like it. Each tree had many branches, the ends of which stretched out like rubber bands trying to connect one to the other. When she looked closer, Mousella noted that each branch pulsed as if alive. The branch endings themselves had oscillating tentacles from which a thin liquid oozed, reminding her of sticky tree sap.

The air was polluted, and the acrid odor noted by all on the raft intensified the farther inland Mousella travelled. The flat trees with their horizontal branches grew into a crawling forest along the ground. The branches had become interlaced, and navigation was arduous. Mousella's eyes stung and her whiskers tingled. She felt apprehensive.

Zzzzzap! Suddenly, one of her precious whiskers was singed when it accidentally grazed one of the tree branch endings. A faint swirl of gray smoke twirled up from the whisker's burned end.

A stunned Mousella screeched out, "Ooooo, ouch, oh my stars! Help! I've been shocked."

The small mouse was terrified and remained motionless for some time. Finally, she took a careful step forward, adapting to the dangers of the landscape by curling up her tail and tucking in her whiskers. She was able to continue exploring but did so with great caution, taking only one step at a time along the convoluted topography of the island.

Eventually Mousella reached a gully that seemed to split the island in half. Afraid to cross the deep divide, she turned to the left. As she went along, the landscape changed, becoming thick with tangled webs and blobs of gunk. She sniffed decay all around. The trees, which once pulsed with life, were withered. Their branch ends were weighted down by a collection of hardened material.

Mousella no longer concerned herself with protecting her whiskers and tail, since the liquid oozing from the branch endings had all but stopped. She could hear an occasional hiss or sputter, but even that finally fizzled out. Then to her utter surprise, Mousella heard a faint moan coming from one of the dark hardened objects at the end of a distant branch. Carefully she crawled over to the moaning object, experiencing a different kind of shock when the blob tried to say something.

"Youcantmehepnomore."

"What did you say?" Mousella asked.

"Youcantmehepnomore."

Mousella still couldn't understand. "Please speak up and say one word at a time."

"You can't me help no more." Then the thing added, "It's loot ate."

Mousella could sense the blob's distress from inflection alone, despite not understanding the individual words. "Can you tell me what's wrong?"

The blob did not answer.

Probing further, Mousella said, "Well, then, who are you? Or should I ask who *were* you?"

"Mnamez Amy and I was a tep in mu tooth 'n so was mu drend, Lloyd therover."

Mousella tried but still couldn't understand. She was about to move on when she was called over by another blob at the end of an adjacent branch. Turning, she saw that this one was struggling to get loose, but each time—Zzzzzap—it would receive another shock from the still active end of one of the tree branches.

Despite this, it began to speak. "My name is Lloyd. Amy, the blob next to me, is my friend. Once we were hamsters, living freely in the wild woods. Because of our good nature, humans began capturing us. They put us into cages and tamed us. We were their teps...I mean, their pets. That's what we were until—well, later. When any of us become forgetful, befuddled, or perceived as useless, we wind up here. It's okay when we first arrive but then, not knowing where to go, we wander around. Inevitably we bump into the tree branches and get zapped. It seems that one zap leads to another as we're bumped from one tree branch to another. Eventually we become dazed, and even though we yell out for help, no one comes. So we wait around, give up, start to die, and harden. It's called Old Hamster's Disease, and it's a rather ignominious way to go."

"That's a very big word," said Mousella. "What does it mean?"

"I guess you can define it as being disgraceful or humiliating. I used to know lots of big words but I've started to forget them."

Mousella was horrified. "How could this happen? It's terrible! Hideous and horrible."

Lloyd continued, "Some of us die and harden right away, while others, like me and Amy, take a while. But she'll be gone soon. You can tell by her speech. And well, it won't be long for me either."

"Can you tell me about the other two islands that are nearby?" Mousella asked.

"Yes, one is like a sinking ship and I'm afraid that the other has, indeed met its fate. It now lies at the bottom of the sea. Collectively we are known as the Isles of Ill."

Mousella wanted to gather as much information as she could for Captain Norton so she asked one more question. "But what makes the islands sink?"

"Well, little mouse, when all of us hamsters harden, the island gets too heavy to float, so it becomes rock solid and sinks."

"Lloyd, I know it's too late for Amy, but is there any way I can help you escape?"

"No, little mouse. Once you've had one too many zaps, it's only a matter of time. This part of the island is already severely damaged. By the way, you haven't been shocked yet, have you?"

"Well, yes, but only once." Mousella was nervous as she showed Lloyd her singed whisker.

"Not good. You've already been marked. And one mark begets another and then another, until it's loot ate. Sorry, I mean too late. Get away from here fast. But first I need to tell you something important."

Lloyd began speaking as quickly as he could. "If you're careful not to touch the ending, you can break off one of the branches and take it with you for tropection... I mean, protection. It must be longer than the width of your whiskers from end to end on both sides. Carry it in your mouth so the branch dends... ends... do the bumping and not you. They'll be zapped instead of your kwiskers... er, whiskers. The island may start sinking by daybreak, so get off as quickly as you can. Go now! And never kool kcab."

Mousella thanked him. "Lloyd, you're a life saver and my hero. Now, I'd better be going."

"Please, one more thing, little mouse, and this is very important, so listen carefully. When the energy end of your branch contacts the energy end of another branch, it'll cause a tolj... I mean jolt. This will thrust you forward. That way, you'll get to the sore you sheek faster. I mean, shore you seek."

"How should I choose a branch?"

"Choose one from around here because they are easier to break off. Don get me grong, they still have 'nough zip, or should I say zap, to boost your journey."

"Thank you! Thank you so much for all your help. I will never ever be able to return the favor."

"I'm the one who should thank you. You've given me a chance to be a friend, if not a tep...I mean, pet...one more time in my pitiful life. It is you who have uplifted me in this time of strife and moiltur...turmoil."

Mousella was in tears as she hugged Lloyd, who wanted to hug her back but couldn't, because his hamster paws were already frozen into hard blobs. She regretfully said her goodbyes to Lloyd and to Amy, who was now completely wordless.

Mousella broke off one of the healthier looking tree branches from the middle, avoiding the energized end just as Lloyd had instructed. Then she held it up for him to see. Faintly she could hear Lloyd yelp out, "Do yiddit."

Examining the stick, Mousella noted that it was gnarled with a bit of green moss and scaly patches. Just as she brought the branch to her mouth, she was startled when it spoke.

"I hear your name is Mousella...translated, that means little mouse. I am so glad you selected me. My name is Embla and I will safely guide you through the forest. When I tell you to touch my energized end to one of the other branch ends, you must do so. Okay?"

Mousella was so astounded that all she could say was, "Okay."

Embla continued her instructions. "Be ready for a quick forward thrust when I touch the other branch. Some of the jolts will take us farther than others, but be assured that you'll get to your shore before daybreak. Ready?"

"I'm ready whenever you are...uh, Elba."

"It's Embla, not Elba," the branch responded.

With Embla securely in Mousella's mouth, they were off, turning this way and that with each jolt. It was a short, wild ride, and they arrived at the exact point along the shore where Mousella had crawled onto the isle.

Mousella stood on the sinking shore, staring into the waning night. Slowly it gave way to a crimson crack on the horizon hinting that daybreak was imminent. The raft was barely distinguishable, enveloped in a mantle of fog.

Mousella took Embla from between her teeth, gently placed the branch on the ground, and took a deep breath. "Well, Embla, we're here. I never would have made it without you. You transported me ever so safely. I am indebted to you and the energy with which you transported me through this strange isle."

"It was my pleasure. I must say, I even surprised myself. I would never have had a chance to use that ol' spark, hahaha, it if it hadn't been for your need."

"Oh, Embla, you are funny. But tell me, where will you go from here?"

"I don't know. If I stay here on the shore, I'll be taken out to sea, when high tide comes, and become a drifter...hahaha. Actually, Mousella, I think I would prefer to come along with you, wherever it is you're headed."

Pointing toward the raft, Mousella asked, "Can you see the raft floating out there in the sea?"

"I can see neither the sea nor your raft," Embla replied.

"I know it's foggy. Squint. Then maybe you can make it out."

"No, you don't understand. I can't squint because I have no eyes."

"What? You're without sight?" Mousella asked in disbelief.

"Yup, I can feel, hear, think, and talk, but I can't see, smell, or taste."

"Then how did you navigate us here across the island?"

"I felt my way. And besides, with my connections and dynamic personality, I can go anywhere, hahaha."

"Wow. That's truly amazing. I wonder if you'll make connections aboard the raft...that is, if you come along."

"So I can come with you? Really? Can I?"

"Sure. Why not? Absolutely. And I'm sure you'll make connections. You know, Embla, you have quite a way with words."

"Well, yes, we branches in the front part of the isle are wordy as well as woody...hahaha. You don't know this, but I have the potential to speak many languages. Perhaps I could be a translator someday."

"Translator? How do you know you can translate?"

"I just know. For one, we branches had to understand the hamsters. I bet you didn't understand Amy when she tried to speak to you."

"You've got that right. What *did* she say?"

"She said, 'You can't help me anymore. It's too late.'"

"Wow, that's an awesome skill. Listen, I'm sure that my raft-mates will be impressed by your talents. I can't wait until you meet Captain Norton and First Mate, Mordecai." Worried, Mousella continued, "Embla, I just thought of something. What if you get wet on the way over?"

"I'll be fine…just need to dry out, that's all. Hey, I promise not to be troublesome. Besides, who knows? Maybe I can even be helpful."

"Embla don't you realize how much you've already helped? I would have sizzled and hardened just like Amy and Lloyd if it hadn't been for you. So, ready? It's my turn to transport you. Let's go."

Again Mousella carefully placed Embla between her teeth. As she entered the cold sea and began swimming toward the raft, Mousella kept her nose as high above the water's surface as possible. Even with her best efforts, Mousella was unable to keep Embla from getting dunked repeatedly.

To make the trip even more difficult, the thick plants that Mousella encountered on her way to the isle became entangled on Embla's ends as Mousella got closer to the raft,. Twisting this way and that, Mousella constantly wiggled to release the seaweed's strong hold. In doing so, some of the plants got in her mouth. And to get rid of the stuff, she chewed and swallowed it.

Despite these difficulties, they finally reached the bow of the raft.

96

~11~

Mousella Returns

"I see her! Here she comes!"

"Me too. I saw her first!"

Sis and Sass yelled back and forth and quickly blinked their dots and dash signals to the skunks and beavers.

Below, all gathered on deck for the sisters' news.

"Attention! Now hear this. Mousella is at the bow," yelled Sis.

"And she's carrying something in her mouth," hollered Sass.

Norton rushed off in the lead, followed by Mordecai, then Celeste, and finally Sis and Sass trailing behind, as they headed for the raft's bow. The rest of the Salvation Seekers remained mid-deck so as not to upset the balance on the raft and cause a tipping point.

Upon reaching the bow, Norton saw that Mousella had already climbed aboard with a stick in her mouth. Mousella was shaking with cold. The little mouse's dark brown fur was matted and still had some of the seaweed clinging to her back. Her whiskers, usually stiff and shiny, were heavy and drooping wet, one of them scorched and shorter than the others. Her eyes, usually bright and alert, were dull. She looked stunned.

Embla hung from Mousella's lax jaw until slowly she fell, landing with a thud onto the deck, where she lay sodden, swollen, and limp.

Norton was the first to speak. "Quick, Sis and Sass, make covers from your silk threads and wrap them around Mousella and this...this...I guess it's a stick of some kind. Mordecai, fetch the hot temp tonic in my lab. It's in the beaker with bubbling red liquid, on the lab table. And be careful."

Sis and Sass fashioned blankets from the silk still atop their backs and covered Mousella and Embla. Mordecai arrived with the tonic, which he carefully handed over to Norton. After cooling the liquid by mixing in a little sea water, Norton administered three drops directly into Mousella's mouth. While he was tending to Mousella, Celeste pulled back the blanket of silk and began applying the oily tonic to Embla's damp form. The moss on Embla began to green up, and the white patches which had faded away began to reemerge.

Once Mousella regained consciousness, she tried to recount the strange story of the Isles of Ill. Because her voice was only a faint whisper, Norton, Mordecai, and Celeste crowded close to hear her words. To them, her story sounded like gibberish.

"Hush now, Mousella. You aren't making any sense. Tell us after you sleep off this weariness and regain your strength. Celeste will take you back to our makeshift den and watch over you until you're strong enough to give a full report."

"But... but Captain, I can't leave Embla."

"What are you talking about? Who is Embla?"

Mousella gathered all the energy she had left in her small weary self and muttered, "The stick. That wet stick next to me. I need her. Embla's my friend. She has to dry out."

With that, Mousella fell back unconscious. Quickly Norton administered a few more drops of the tonic and rubbed some of the warm, musky liquid onto the top of Mousella's head. Celeste then carried Mousella to their 'den.'

Once Mousella was taken away, Embla sensed the absence of her new friend and began to panic. She cried out, "Little mouse, where are you? Don't abandon me."

Those within hearing distance were thunderstruck.

"By the might of the waters below and the sky above, this stick has spoken." Mordecai approached. "Are you the one Mousella calls Embla?"

"Yes, that would be me. Please don't separate us. Take me to Mousella, I beg you."

Norton said, "Embla, I'm Norton Bulymur, Captain of the Salvation Seekers. Clearly, something astonishing has happened between our Mousella and you during her explorations. We shall let you dry out alongside your new friend Mousella. Perhaps by sundown you both can give us a full accounting. Now daybreak is upon us and we all need to rest."

That evening, Norton summoned Mousella and Embla to his lab space. The now inseparable friends recounted the horrors of the Isles of Ill to the captain and first mate.

"Embla, we're so grateful to you for guiding our dear Mousella through the forest maze," said Norton. "Please accept our deepest gratitude."

"Thank you for allowing me to remain with Mousella, Captain. I am at your service."

Turning to Mousella, Norton said, "My dear friend, I want you to know how very proud Mordecai and I are. Your bravery in the face of great danger will never be forgotten, and your explorations were essential to our wellbeing. Your adventure will be included in *The Saga of the Skunk Salvation Seekers*, which I am writing for all the future generations in our family and extended family to read."

"Ah, Captain, it was the least I could do after all you've done for me. However, without the help of Lloyd Hamster, I never would have made it off the island. I would have become petrified and perished along with the others, stuck in that dreadful place forever. It was his secret about the branches that led me to Embla. I owe him a debt of gratitude which can never be repaid." Mousella began to sniffle. "And I'm sad because he couldn't be saved."

Mousella began to cry and then sob. It was Embla who provided words of consolation.

"Mousella, I understand your grief. But think of it this way: even though you weren't able to save Lloyd, you saved me, and I surely would have suffered the same sinking fate. If it had not been for you, I would now be petrified. There were many branches to select from, and yet you chose me. When you broke me away from the others, you released me from an inevitable sentence that would have shriveled my existence. Without my help, you would never have reached the raft before the island's demise. Our meeting was fortuitous, and our relationship reciprocal. We owe that to Lloyd. Bless you, Lloyd...and Amy, too."

There was a moment of silence after Embla spoke, Then the captain invited Embla to join their family of Salvation Seekers, which by now included more than just skunks.

"Listen, Captain Norton, as it is presently I'm but a worthless stick, a branch, a mere twig. I have little to offer."

"Well, you could be a cane or a pole or a rod," suggested Mordecai.

"Yes, I could serve those functions, but they are rather static responsibilities. I was born to be dynamic. You see, my power end still has some verve, if you know what I mean...kick. I just need to find a new energy source with which to unite—like a match. Then I'll be up to speed in no time. And then, *vavavoom*."

"Yup, you should have seen how really, truly—and I mean very fast—Embla got me from inside the island to shorcline. It was amazing. She can go like a whiz."

Mordecai stroked his white whiskers, pondering the discussion. "Hmmm, well that's a splendid attribute. I must give this further thought... Yes, wow!"

"There's even more that Embla can do. Go, on Embla. Tell Captain Norton and Mordecai about your flair for languages."

"It's true, I do have a flair, but everyone on the raft already understands one another."

"Yes, but don't forget what I told you about how Captain Norton and Mordecai want to find a new home in a new land for all the Salvation Seekers. When we get there, we may need an interpreter."

"Look Embla, you're welcome among us even if you have nothing to contribute right now. Your role will eventually be revealed. What we do know now is that the Isles of Ill cannot be our new homeland. It's a source of vile disease and sickness. It's uninhabitable. The faster we depart, the better. However, we can't leave until we solve two problems."

"What would those be, Captain Norton?"

"First, Embla, we have a food shortage problem. And second, First Mate Mordecai still needs to invent a new motion method, so as you can see—"

"Captain Norton," Mousella interrupted, "I think I know where we can get more food. It's easy. Some of the sea's weed got stuck in my mouth when I swam back to the raft. I couldn't spit it out because of Embla, so I swallowed it. Because of the seaweed I had enough energy to complete the expedition without suffering any negative effects."

Norton and Mordecai's eyes met in a simultaneous ah-hah moment.

"You didn't get sick?"

"Not at all."

"Well, Mousella, that confirms it."

"Confirms what, Mordecai?"

"That what you swallowed is safe to eat."

"Oh, did you think the seaweed might be poisonous?"

"We weren't sure, so as an experiment, Captain Norton asked me to eat some, but I haven't had time."

Both the captain and first mate were ecstatic and began whooping and hollering with absolute glee.

"Mordecai, we need to harvest as much of this weed as possible. I'll ask Celeste and her kitchen crew to develop some recipes. Perhaps it'll be seaweed soup for lunch,"

"And," Mordecai added, "seaweed stew for dinner. Yum!"

"Mousella, what a discovery you've made. Do you realize you've solved our food-shortage problem?"

"Captain Norton, it was just by accident."

"Well, not all accidents are discoveries, but many discoveries are accidents."

"I never thought of it that way."

"And," continued Norton, "I must say that you, my brave friend, are worthy of acclaim. We must hold a party in your honor."

Embarrassed, and not wanting to take all the credit for discovering the new food source, Mousella squeaked, "Just a minute, Captain. If Embla hadn't been in my mouth, I might have spit out the seaweed. So you should honor her as well."

"Mousella's right, Captain Norton." Mordecai, who had been listening to the conversation, finally spoke up. "They both deserve to be recognized. Now all we need to worry about is finding a new motion method."

So Norton and Mordecai hurried off to the kitchen to tell Celeste about the new food source and to prepare for a party, leaving Mousella and Embla to themselves.

~ 12 ~

Just the Right Spark

Embla thanked Mousella for sharing the spotlight, and then went on to say, "But my aspirations are such that by using the nerve still within me, I feel sure that I, too, could really be deserving of recognition. But how? If only I were able to unite with a connector, I might be able to solve that other problem mentioned by Mordecai"

"Embla, you mean finding a new motion method?"

"Yes, precisely. Then I would really become a valuable member of the Salvation Seekers instead of just...well, just sticking around, hahaha."

Mousella stroked her whiskers, wiggled her nose, wrinkled the fur above her eyes, and then said, "Hmmm, wait just a minute, Embla. I have an idea. Listen to this: Captain Norton has been experimenting with some hush-hush solution of his. I know because I overheard him talking about it with Mordecai He's sure the skunks can use it as a weapon of defense."

"How does the experiment work?"

"First Captain Norton drinks this liquid potion and gets all bloated. Then he expels it out his…well you know…"

"His posterior?"

"Thanks, Embla, you always have just the right word. Thing is, he needs to know how much of the stuff to drink."

"Oooo, Mousella, I'm beginning to absorb what you're saying. Is there more? Can you start from the beginning?"

"Yes, here it goes. The long and short of the tale is that Captain Norton was born stripeless and became a chemist while trying to develop a solution to make himself stripes. He experimented with many different chemicals and unfortunately burned down his lab, causing such bad pollution in the forest that all the skunks were banished."

"Keep going, I want to know more about it."

"Okay, well, Mordecai, who is an inventor, is Captain Norton's cousin. It was Mordecai who came up with the idea of using a raft for the skunks' get-away. And it was Mordecai who talked the beavers into building the raft. After that, the beavers joined the cause."

"Is there more to the story?"

"Well, yes, lots…but I'll tell you the rest later."

"Mousella, that's interesting, but please do expound upon the experiments themselves."

"Huh?"

"Tell me, please, more about Captain Norton's experiments." Embla rolled back and forth on the deck.

"Okay, Embla, but calm down. You seem to be getting nervous."

"I can't help it. This is just phenomenal."

"He's been practicing ways to control how the gas comes out."

"You mean emissions?"

"If you say so. He wants to be able to release the liquid in either a spray or a stream."

"Is that all?"

"There's more. He's also trying to see how far the gas will squirt and how long each discharge lasts."

As the details of Norton's experiments were revealed, Embla became increasingly animated. Finally in an excited frenzy, she began to shake and then abruptly barked, "That's it! The new energy source. Captain Norton's gas is the essential component required to make this raft whoosh like the wind. Well, hahaha, there hasn't been any wind lately, so I deduce that with my spark in combination—or should I say in combustion with—Captain Norton's gas, a new motion method might come to fruition."

"Embla, you use such big words, I'm not sure I understood all you just said, but I think it was about the possibility of a new way to move the raft forward."

"That's precisely what I meant, little mouse."

"Let's go tell Captain Norton and Mordecai about your idea immediately."

"This scheme will completely shift Norton's paradigm."

"Paradigm?"

"Way of thinking."

"Oh, way of thinking...yeah, I really get it now, don't I?"

Mousella picked up Embla and scampered off to find Norton and Mordecai.

Back in the makeshift galley, while Norton explained the nutritional value of the seaweed to Celeste, Mordecai sat in a corner deep in thought. He had been preoccupied ever since leaving the lab. Celeste gathered her helpers, and they left to harvest the new food source.

After they were gone, Mordecai said, "Norty, I think I've figured out something."

"Figured out what?"

"Well, you know how I've been mulling over finding a new motion method?"

"Yes, of course. It's a tough problem."

"Well, you've been experimenting with the strength and amount of your skunk solution for defense purposes ever since we left the forest. But based on something Embla mentioned earlier, I'm thinking that your gas might have an additional value."

"The gas can do more? What do you mean, Mordy? I've finally perfected emission control and can allow the gas to explode all at once, just a small amount at a time, in a spray, or as a single stream. Not only that, I can make each squirt last over a minute. I've pretty much finished perfecting our first real means of defense. Now I've got to write a training manual before we find a new homeland."

"Listen, Norty, we won't find any land, much less a new homeland, if we don't get this raft moving again. Just think back to what Embla said."

After giving some thought Norton shook his head. "Okay, I give up; what did she say?"

"She said, and I quote, 'All I need to go like the wind, is an energy source with which to unite.' Why not try out your gas for this purpose? If it works the way I envision it, the resulting power can be used to establish a new motion method."

"My stars! It never occurred to me that my gas could be used for any other purpose than defense. Maybe you're right, Mordy. Imagine that...a raft powered by my gas. But how would it work?"

Mousella and Embla arrived at the galley entrance just in time to hear Captain Norton's question.

"Please, may we come in?" Mousella squeaked. "There's something important that Embla and I need to discuss with you."

Mordecai responded, "Perfect timing, we also have something we want to discuss. We need privacy, so let's all go over to my work space."

The four hurried over to Mordecai's space, where they collectively discussed the details of their individual thoughts. As they busily thrashed out the how, why, whereas and if's of a new motion method, Mordecai busily sketched blueprints.

"Okay, let's go over the blueprints," Norton said. "If I understand them correctly, this first print shows me climbing on Brenston Beaver's back."

"Correct, Norty."

Norton continued. "The second print shows that we both have our hind ends facing out toward the sea. The third print shows Brenston tilted backwards with his tail in the water and I'm tilted as well with my hind end close to the water. This fourth print shows Mousella standing next to us with Embla in her mouth and it looks like Embla's energy end is pointed toward my bottom.

"So far, so good, Norty."

"Finally, the fifth and last print shows a spark igniting the gas as I let it out."

"That's absolutely correct. So that, my friends, should cause the raft to move forward, establishing a new motion method," said Mordecai.

The four were ecstatic, jumping up and down as they imagined the "end" result—all except for Embla, who, rather than jumping up and down, was rolling back and forth on the floor. They couldn't wait to try it.

Later that evening, Norton called a meeting of all passengers and crew. He explained the details of Mordecai and Embla's new motion method. The beaver crew heartily approved with much loud tail thumping. The captain decided that they would reconvene the next evening to try out the proposed new method.

All huddled on the deck awaiting the inauguration of the new motion method. At the stern were Norton, Brenston, Mousella, and Embla. Norton sat atop Brenston and both had their hind ends pointed toward the sea. Mousella, facing forward, held Embla in her mouth, with Embla's energy end directed toward Norton's behind. All was readied just as Mordecai had drafted.

Brenston dunked his tail into the cold sea with the uncomfortably bloated Norton upon his back. Mousella, positioned next to Brenston, quivered as she tried to steady Embla, who was all set for ignition. Under the direction of Beatoven, the beavers thumped their tails in a unified fanfare and Mordecai counted.

"A one, and a two, and a three...go."

Norton began to release some of his internal gas, just as Embla discharged a spark from her energy end. A blue flame shot out, and the successful ignition sent the raft thrusting forward with a whoosh.

A wild cheer went up from all aboard.

Sis and Sass climbed their poles to resume look out duties and tend to their sails. The beavers took up their rowing positions, now properly outfitted with protective tail coverings spun by Sis and Sass according to Mordecai's design.

The motion problem was solved at last. By using a combination of the three motion methods — rowing power, wind power, and gas power — the raft was propelled forward on its journey.

~ 13 ~

A Really Big Thing

The troupe traveled effectively from winter into spring, by which time Norton and Celeste had become a family of seven, with three male kits and two female kits. In fact, all the skunks had paired off, mated, bred, and significantly increased the population of the Salvation Seekers. Fortunately, Mordecai had made the raft large enough to accommodate the population growth by at least one generation, so there was still enough room. As for food, they had stored enough of the seaweed to last indefinitely, and Celeste had created many new recipes to delight their palates.

Mordecai continued charting the night sky. But his curiosity did not end with the stars and the moon. He became intrigued by the big round ball he witnessed during the dawning of each new day. So while Norton, Celeste, and the rest of the crew began their daily slumber, Mordecai remained awake, watching the sun as it rose in the sky. He noted that the brightness of the sun chased away the blackness of the night and with it the stars and moon. It bothered him that he couldn't figure out where the moon went during the day or where the sun went during the night.

So Mordecai made up a story which he told to the new kits at the end of the night, just before dawn. The skunk kits and their parents would gather around as "Uncle Mordy" told them his made-up story of Prince Gold and Princess Silver. The kits, wide-eyed and pleading in unison, would say, "Please, Uncle Mordy, tell us just one more time."

And Mordecai would clear his throat before beginning and say, "Okay, just one more time, then off to sleep you go.

"Long, long ago, at the beginning of time, there was a beautiful princess in love with a handsome prince. She was shy and as cool as an evening breeze, while he was bold and as warm as a summer day. Each evening the princess would rise up from her sleeping place, dress in silver, and reveal a little more of her face to the prince. Finally, after thirty nights, her full, round, rosy face could be seen at dusk, just peeking above the line where the sky meets the Earth. Gaining confidence she lost her blush and could be seen, silvery white, traveling high in the sky, looking for Prince Gold.

"When Prince Gold saw Princess Silver shine in all her glory, he fell in love at once and began to seek her out. But it was too late, for she had grown tired and retreated back to her sleeping place. Prince Gold spent the day hunting across the sky in search of his love, but alas, he also grew tired and retreated to his sleeping place. Thus they chased each other across the sky, Princess Silver by night and Prince Gold by day, never catching up to one another, for she was a night princess and he was a day prince. The End."

* * *

As spring progressed into summer, all was proceeding in the usual manner — so much so, that life on board the raft had become mundane. Sis and Sass were more argumentative. The beavers, goaded by Beatoven, were more demanding. Norton worked tirelessly writing his manual on the control, emission, and ethical use of skunk stink, ignoring Celeste who was too busy tending their kits to even notice. And Mordecai, who had shed his heavier white winter fur for a sleeker brown summer look, seemed edgy. There was a subtle restlessness aboard the NBC Barge. Only Mousella and Embla were content with their routine.

On the eve of another night, like so many that had passed before, the beavers, as had become their ritual, gathered at the stern of the raft for a meeting of the Brotherhood during one of their breaks.

Beatoven began the meeting. "Fellow Brotherhood members, why's it taking such a long time to git where we need to be? We need to be where we need to be, wherever that is, but we need to git there soon. I don't see none of yous paired off, mated, or in a family way. We's gotta have lives too."

In unison the beavers thumped their tails and repeated, "We's gotta have lives too."

Beatoven continued, "Just how much longer will this trip take?"

Defending Norton, Brenston spoke up. "Don't forget, Beats, that when Embla lights Captain Norton's gas, it sure propels us forward faster."

In a huff, Beatoven retorted, "I know, Brenston. You may have the captain on your back, but it's our rears in the water, not his."

Again the beavers thumped their tails and cheered. "Not his rear in the water, not his." They were becoming agitated when suddenly a loud, low, rumbling sound cut through the rising tension. It was accompanied by an unexpected cloudburst, which drenched the beavers.

"Ah, for the love of our rivers. I never heard such a scary thunder."

The deep roar continued, followed by high-pitched squeals and another misty downpour.

The beavers were hurriedly dispersing when Norton appeared mid-deck along with Celeste, the other skunks, their kits, Mordecai, Mousella, and Embla.

"No, don't go. Stay where you are. Sis and Sass have signaled an emergency. They've been blinking wildly, and I expect they'll be here soon with a broadcast."

Within seconds the sisters scuttled in on their sixteen legs as fast as they could. Out of breath and looking more alarmed than ever before, they gasped as they spoke each word.

"We've...just seen...the most amazing thing.". It was Sis who was the first to speak followed by Sass.

"Yeah... more amazing even... than the Isles of Ill."

"It's another... island... but this time... it appeared out of nowhere... just rising up out of the sea."

"Yeah, and there are two holes on top of the island... some kind of volcano, I suppose.

"Listen, Sis, you weren't the only one to see the holes... I saw them too. And I even saw a huge white mist shoot out of one of them."

The spiders' underbellies were bright red, and their eyes looked as I if they might pop right out of their small heads.

"Ladies, calm down," Norton interrupted. "Catch your breath. We all heard a very scary loud noise. Did it come from this new island?"

The sisters eyed each other and continued their story, after taking a few large breaths.

"Yes, Captain Norton, with each spray coming from the hole, there was a loud roar."

"It was low pitched and lasted a long time."

"We heard it too," Beatoven announced. "It was a spooky growling sound. And then we got wet, probably from that spray Sis and Sass just told us about."

The words *volcano, roar, growling,* and *spooky,* set the Salvation Seekers into a frenzy of concern. Mordecai, sensing that Norton did not know what to do, spoke up next.

"Now everybody, let's all get back to work. Sis and Sass will keep us updated. Go on now, go on... no need for undue alarm."

However, only Sis and Sass left to resume lookout duties since the crew and passengers insisted on continuous reports. The rest of the troupe remained fixed to their spots, murmuring to one another as they tried to fathom what had happened, and what might happen next.

It wasn't long before Sis and Sass again scrambled down from their posts to update the others. As was usual, Sis spoke first, to the annoyance of Sass.

"It's fully emerged and it's not an island, it's a...a *Thing*."

"You're right, Sis, this *Thing* is definitely not an island."

Norton, visibly impatient, drew up on his hind legs to make himself appear larger than the other animals on deck. "Sisters, please. Make yourselves clear. What is this, uh...Thing you're talking about?"

Sis answered, "Captain Norton, Sass and I don't know what else to call it, so we just call it *Thing*."

"Okay, but can you describe this thing?"

"Yes, it's mostly dark gray with huge white flippers, an enormous tail, and as we described before, it has two holes on its back from which it blows mist and makes noise."

Then Sass concluded, "Captain Norton, I think *Thing* might be some kind of monstrous fish."

"Sis, where do you think we can best see this thing, or fish, as you suggest?" Norton asked.

"I think probably over toward the front of the raft."

Immediately Norton headed to the raft's bow, followed by Mordecai, who was followed by

Celeste, who was followed by Mousella, who was followed by a rolling Embla, who was followed by all the rest. The raft, heavy with unequal distribution, began to tilt and would have capsized had it not been for a timely event, the appearance of the thought-to-be-lost-at-sea beavers, Barclay and Benjamin.

~ 14 ~

A Whale of a Tale

"Hey, Subby, look over there. It's the raft we been telling you 'bout. We're getting closer," Barclay hollered to the great sea beast, Subbaldus.

Subbaldus, open-mouthed, was swimming above the choppy surface of the ocean, while the two lost-at-sea beavers were seated on their own tails upon the floor of the beast's mouth.

"I think I can just make out Brenston," Barclay said to Benjamin. "And is that Beats?"

"Don't know," replied Benjamin.

Only Sis and Sass had witnessed the presumed demise of Barclay and Benjamin in the storm that blew the raft to the Isles of Ill. All the others on board had been bound up and asleep, the result of their sedating spider bites. When the misfortune occurred, Sis and Sass had been wrong. It was Subbaldus, coming up for a breath of fresh air. As he snorted, a gush had exploded from one of the two great nostrils atop his head, causing a spray that shot straight up into the air at the same time the beavers were thrown overboard by the strong wind. Barclay and Benjamin had landed on the very top of Subbaldus's nasal spurt. There they remained precariously suspended, face down, with their bellies tickled by foamy bubbles until the vertical spray subsided. When it was over the two beavers had found themselves flattened against a gray wet surface.

Despite being unnerved and confused, the beavers had giggled from the sheer titillation of the event, which was more like an amusement park ride than a terrifying incident.

"Oooh, what was that about?"

"I dunno, Barc, but it sure was a fun thrill. My stomach's doing flip flops."

"Same here, it's a weird feeling, ain't it?"

Then the intoxication of the experience wore off, and their first instinct was to regain balance. Using their flat tails for support, Barclay and Benjamin attempted to take a step or two.

"Be careful," Barclay warned Benjamin. "It's awful slippery."

The beavers were unable to adjust to Subbaldus's slick, smooth back. They fumbled, tripped, and then fell headfirst down one of the blowholes, Barclay followed by Benjamin.

"Whoa, what's goin' on here? Where are we? And how come I'm sliding?"

"Don't know, Barc, but wherever we're at, it's twisting and turning. And the sides are kind of bumpy."

Their tails thumped as they slid down Subbaldus's trachea, the inner rings acting both as speed bumps slowing down the velocity of their fall and as musical bars producing accidental notes as the flat of their tails slapped each rung, mallet style, producing a rhythmic tune.

Then bump, bump, bumpety-bump, Barclay bounced a few times hitting the bottom of a space that was both expansive and stretchy.

A not-so-far-off voice, amplified by the tube, yelled, "Hey, Barc, look out. I'm right behind you."

Then bump, bump, bumpety-bump, Benjamin bounced in next to Barclay.

"It's dark in here," said Benjamin.

"Yeah, but ya know, I feel like it's real airy."

"Let's walk around...see where we're at."

"Hey, Ben, them walls feel stretchy."

"They sure do. I'm thinking it's some kinda balloon...Whoa! Now what's happenin'?"

The great fish started another blow, and its lungs, containing the two beavers, began to contract.

"The walls, they're closing in," yelled Barclay.

"We gotta get out of here."

Barclay and Benjamin quickly climbed back up, this time using the trachea rungs as they would a ladder, until reaching the opening into which they had originally fallen. Carefully they crawled out of the hole and emerged into the night.

Within moments of surfacing, Barclay and Benjamin again started the slip-and-slide fun.

"Hold on, here we go again."

This time, instead of slipping back down one of the blowholes, they began to slide up and then down the curve of Subbaldus's back which, to them, seemed like a great hill.

"Whee, whoo, wow, meet ya soon," screamed Benjamin to Barclay who was directly in front of him also squealing and hollering as they slid toward the rear of the sea beast.

The last thing they saw before being flipped into the water, directly in front of the sea beast's great mouth, was the largest fish tail they'd ever seen. Subbaldus opened his expansive lips for what he thought would be a fine supper. His great tongue lapped out, scooped up Barclay and Benjamin, and then thrust them into his immense mouth where they came to rest upon the top of Subbaldus's rough tongue.

The great fish puckered and then smacked his lips while wondering what had just passed through his food portal. This wasn't the usual school of krill. The two, of whatever they were, felt somewhat fuzzy and not worth swallowing, but because Subbaldus was curious, he didn't spit them out.

Instead he asked, in a great deep voice, "What is this? What fish or animal type are you who have entered my mouth?"

The beavers, despite the unknown danger of their precarious situation, greeted the strange experience with uncontrollable laughter. Benjamin and Barclay had doubled over in fits of hilarity until the great sea beast began to speak. They were just catching their breath when the tongue of the sea beast, upon which they were seated, began to move. Barclay and Benjamin were then abruptly thrown from the floor of Subbaldus's mouth to the roof. Next they were thrashed front to back and side to side as Subbaldus asked his thunderous questions. Caught in an echo chamber, they cowered as the interrogation reverberated against the arched, cave-like, interior walls of Subbaldus's oral cavity.

"What is this-is-is? What fish-ish-ish or animal type-ipe-ipe are you-oo-oo who have entered my mouth-outh-outh?"

The two beavers looked at one another in wonderment, not yet realizing that they had been swallowed and were inside the mouth of a great sea beast.

"Ben, who, or what, was that?"

"I dunno. Loudest voice I ever did hear. Sounded like there was more than one."

"Where we at?"

"Must be inside something's mouth because that's what it said."

"I'm scared, Ben."

"Me too, Barc. Should we answer?"

Again Subbaldus asked, "Who enters my mouth-outh-outh? Are you food or foe-oh-oh?"

Barclay, gathering up his nerve finally spoke. "Us two are beavers. Who are you?"

"I am the greatest sea animal to swim the seven seas. My name is Subbaldus-aldus-aldus."

"Well, hey there, Subbaldus, I'm Barclay and this here's my friend, Benjamin. You can call us Barc and Ben. I don't know if we're friends, but we're not no foes."

"Then you might as well be friends-ends-ends, since beavers don't appeal to my tastes nor to my stomach-ock-ock. How did you happen to be here, out in the open seas-eez-eez, so far away from home-ome-ome?"

Barclay and Benjamin explained their misadventures to Subbaldus who listened intently to the strange story.

After Subbaldus understood the beavers' plight, he agreed to use his navigational skills to help Barclay and Benjamin find their raft. He even volunteered to deliver all aboard the NBC Barge to a new homeland.

Until they were reunited with the rest of the passengers, Barclay and Benjamin had remained safe and warm inside Subbaldus's mouth. Subbaldus kept his mouth as tightly shut as a deadbolt lock while traveling through the depths of the sea and only opened wide when breaking the surface to breathe. It was then that Barclay and Benjamin were able to scan the horizon searching for captain, crew, and all their raft-mates.

It took many suns and many moons before Subbaldus located the NBC Barge. The great sea beast had been skimming along the surface of the sea when he heard Barclay holler, "Hey Subby, look over there. It's the raft we been telling you 'bout."

No sooner had Subbaldus noted the distant raft, than he also noted its tilting motion and knew that disaster was about to befall the small vessel and its inhabitants. He closed his mouth, encasing Barclay and Benjamin in waterproof safety, and dove underwater, swimming as quickly as he could. Using his internal sonar detection system, Subbaldus resurfaced in front of the raft just as the tilting pressure tore the reeds that held the logs together. The raft began to break apart as the animals, including Captain Norton and First Mate Mordecai

124

slid down the tilted bow of the NBC Barge directly onto Subbaldus's tongue. He flicked them backward into his massive oral cavity where they were joyfully reunited with Barclay and Benjamin.

The new surroundings provided by Subbaldus were large enough to accommodate all passengers of the now destroyed NBC Barge, which had sunk to the bottom of the sea.

Since the beavers no longer had to row, they were able to rest. Sis and Sass relinquished their duties as watch-spiders, but continued to bicker nonetheless. Norton and Celeste were able to spend more quality time with each other and their kits. Mousella spent time exploring the whale's mouth, including his huge teeth, on which she discovered edible moss. Embla practiced her language skills, realizing that when Subbaldus spoke, the shape of his oral cavity created an echo chamber, making it sound like there was more than one sea beast.

Only First Mate Mordecai was dissatisfied. He missed his work space. And he was lonely. With Norton spending more time with Celeste and their offspring, Mordecai knew that he would need to find a mate for himself once they settled in a new homeland. He hoped there would be weasels in this, yet, unknown place.

Subbaldus kept his promise in assisting the Salvation Seekers to find a new home. Diving under again, with his new friends harbored within, he resumed his sea travel, heading east toward a distant shore.

When he was within a whale's eye view of land, Subbaldus surfaced, opened his large mouth, and stuck out his very long tongue. The animals took turns diving off his springy appendage. Crew members went first, some diving headfirst and others leaping tail first. Celeste led the skunk families, holding their kits above the waves. Then Sis, Sass, and Mousella leaped into the calm waters. Finally, Captain Norton and First Mate Mordecai dove into the ocean, joining the rest of the Salvation Seekers.

With a flick of his massive tail creating a new wave, Subbaldus propelled the Salvation Seekers forward.

Epilogue

Dazed and disoriented, the animals landed on a shore somewhere along America's Eastern Seaboard. The landscape was not unlike the one from which they had escaped, both with rocky shorelines and thick forests in the distance. Because these like vistas lent a sense of familiarity, causing temporary consternation, readers can only guess how long it took each of the Salvation Seekers to realize they had indeed arrived at a new home and new beginning.

In time, the raft's inhabitants dispersed, scattering in all directions, ready for adventure and discovery. What they found were magnificent landscapes — some lush with plants, others barren, stark, and rugged. Naturally the beavers sought out forest streams and woodland lakes, glad for the opportunity to once again return to dam and den building. The skunks, now many in number, traveled throughout the dense forests, which had a variety of timbers and earthen floors carpeted with more colors than can be imagined by the reader.

The sky, with its multicolored splendor at dusk and dawn, continued to delight the animals, as did the brightness of the sun and moon. White clouds matched the purity of the snow and were perfectly reflected on shimmering lake waters. When the clouds were dark, prepared to cool the land with clean rain and quench the thirst of the land's inhabitants, the inland waters were colored gray and dark. All was pure, all was fresh, all was perfection, and the animals thrived.

So, what happened to Norton and Celeste, to Mordecai, to Sis and Sass, to Brenston and Beathoven, to Mousella and Embla?

Celeste brought up the kits, readying them for their skunk stage of maturity. She guarded the acorn necklace housing its secret formula for skunk stink. And they, along with Mordecai and his newfound mate, traveled inland, finally settling in a wonderful place where the forests were thick with streams tumbling over rocks and where, nearby, three large rivers joined together. It was here that Norton furthered his experiments on the control of skunk musk and how to use it responsibly, authoring several important works of skunk nonfiction, notably *Saga of the Skunk Salvation Seekers*, *The Control and Use of Skunk Stink*, and *The Skunk's Art of Defense*.

Together, he and Celeste developed the Mephitidae Code of Honor, later known as The Three Rs of Respect, Responsibility, and Resolution.

As for Sis and Sass, they stayed together, never remarrying but continuing to tease and taunt one another throughout their lives. Brenston and Beathoven, who never agreed with one another, parted ways for streams in opposite directions of the woodlands where they each headed up building projects but with very different management styles.

And finally, Mousella and Embla remained in-separable. Ultimately all the characters were swept away by many generations, except for one, and that was Embla, who entered a dormant spell to be awak-ened at some distant time during the Age of Aquarius.

* * *

So what did destiny hold for our dear animals and animal friends, as well as the land upon which they lived out their long and fruitful lives? Readers who want to learn what happened to the progeny of the original Skunk Salvation Seekers, far into the future by many generations, will find their furry adventuresome friends again in *Sebastian's Tale*.

About Dylan Weiss

Dylan, a speech-language pathologist for more than thirty-five years, specialized in geriatric communication disorders and progressive neurologic disease. When her mother developed Parkinson's and could not get treatment due to misunderstood Medicare regulations, she was inspired to make a difference by writing *Reimbursable Geriatric Service Delivery, a Functional Maintenance Therapy System*, which became a bestseller in her profession.

After her husband was diagnosed with Alzheimer's disease, Dylan retired from a successful career and became a caregiver for the next fifteen years. Again, she was inspired to write, documenting the challenges they faced and the creative communication programs she developed throughout his decline. Dylan's article, "Sharing the Load," won an Excel Award from the Society of National Association of Publishers in the literary category.

After Dave's death, Dylan became a community leader, sitting on Parks and Recreation boards, improving the township's parks system, promoting green efforts, and expanding her writing efforts. *Norton's Tale* is a prequel to her chapter book, *Sebastian's Tale*. Look for the third book in her Skunk Tales Trilogy in the future.

Dylan's hope is that readers of *Norton's Tale* are inspired to make a difference by daring to dream.

Visit Dylan on the web at: www.SebastiansTale.com.

www.ingramcontent.com/pod-product-compliance
Lightning Source LLC
Chambersburg PA
CBHW060427260626
47161CB00005B/1816